AN LA TO LA COZY MYSTERY BOOK 2

Bad Blood
in the Bayou

'WIDE-ANGLE'

JULIE BELMONT

Bad Blood in the Bayou

WIDE-ANGLE

Julie Belmont

NIGHT RAVEN PUBLISHING

eBook ISBN: 978-0-9755984-5-0

Paperback ISBN: 978-0-9755984-6-7

Cover Design by: Julie Belmont

Cover Art by: Julie Belmont Original Acrylic Painting—Wedding Bayou

Printed in the United States of America

Published by: Night Raven Publishing

I dedicate this book to:

My daughter Krystle who is my Eternal Inspiration
Love you Forever and Always till Eternity and Beyond

Contents

Chapter 1

Fairy Tale Wedding

This assignment is one I know I'm going to enjoy, judging from such a picturesque and magnificent backdrop. The wedding that will be spoken of for years will take place here in a month. I am honored to have the opportunity to immortalize it with my photography. The opulence of this home is that of a fairy tale. The two-story mansion with a wrap-around balcony on the top floor and a wrap-around veranda on the bottom with elaborate wrought iron is picture-perfect. From where I stand, it looks like a gigantic and enchanting wedding cake. The setting is ideal, though it took me about forty minutes to drive across the Lake Pontchartrain Causeway. The twenty-three-mile bridge is one way to get from the primary waterfront in New Orleans straight across north to the prestigious town of Mandeville.

I remember meeting Mr. Eugene Fontaine and his charming and beautiful wife, Olivia, and their handsome son, Ethan, though somewhat shy. The benefit ball they hosted was to raise money for one of their many charities. The family, which has roots in France and Spain, came to New Orleans four generations ago. Their diligent hard work, kindness to employees, and benevolence have made them royalty in the town. Their financial wealth is surpassed only by their joy in life and their grateful and nurturing nature to all who meet them. A simple meeting, a shake of a hand, and a gracious promise that maybe one day they would welcome my services have come full circle. I now stand here, ready to walk up to this beautiful residence and become part of the most glorious, happy event: the wedding of their first son, Ethan Fontaine, to the lovely Jane Douth.

One of the double doors opens, and I'm met with a gregarious little lady in her early fifties. She's trying not to be outdone by the little fluffy dog at her feet, who has a helicopter prop for a tail. Smiling widely, she apologizes for the little dog and welcomes me simultaneously. Have I passed through a porthole to an alternative super-happy universe?

"Hi, I'm Jessica, the photographer. I have an appointment to meet with Mrs. Olivia Fontaine." I say as I watch Olivia running down the stairs with arms stretched out in a ready-to-hug position. Again, the feeling of an alternative universe.

"Welcome, Jessica, to our home, and thank you, Anne." She says, graciously acknowledging the lady who let me in. She continues, "Anne, would you be so kind as to prepare some iced tea, or would you prefer lemonade?" She asks, looking in my direction.

"Lemonade sounds great."

"Anne, please bring a pitcher of lemonade to the back patio. Thank you, dear," Olivia says as she moves towards the back of the house. She's wearing a lovely white outfit, a silk-like tank top, matching wide-leg pants tied at the waist, and a floral see-through overcoat flowing behind her like a summer breeze.

She motions with her elegant hand for me to sit in the most inviting and comfortable chair imaginable. Of course, as the city's, if not the nation's, most renowned designer, her home is a testament to perfect decoration. At the same time, it is warm and comfortable.

"I must apologize, as my son Ethan and his fiancée Jane will not be joining us for this meeting," she says nervously, which somehow seems foreign to her initial demeanor.

"Not a problem, we can go over the initial details. In our phone conversation, you mentioned the wedding would take place here. You can show me around, and I can take notes on the best locations for the photographs. Would you know how many will be at the wedding party?"

"Not sure how that will work out. My son has many friends; although he is naturally shy, he is loved by many. The majority of his friends he has known most of his life. Some attended Tulane University with him. By contrast, Jane is an orphan; her parents died in a tragic car accident. I don't know the details; she refuses to talk about it. If anyone asks questions, she reacts emotionally and usually runs out of the room crying. We have no idea how old Jane was when it happened. Or how long ago it took place. As far as Jane goes, it seems it happened yesterday. We tried to find out something about it. Maybe knowing what happened would help us understand and help her deal with the loss. It seems like all records of the accident just vanished."

"What you're saying is the typical shot of the groom's men and the bridesmaids' photograph may be unevenly proportioned. I like taking pictures that transcend time and give the bride and groom wonderful, lasting memories. Whatever, that is for the individual couple."

"I'm glad you're a visionary and able to adapt to the situation." She says, reaching out and tapping my hand. Her warmth is as charming as her smile, but her eyes betray her somehow. I hope to be interpreting a bit of stress, not apprehension.

"Jane needs to be surrounded by loving, welcoming family and friends. This joyous event will give her that. It may seem odd, but I would like to take a picture of all who will be gathered-- with them in the middle, front row, and center. That way, she'll know how much love will always surround her."

"That will be lovely, but we have about 100 people attending. Can you get them all around the happy couple?"

"Not a problem. I have the wide-angle lens to die for."

Chapter 2

First Impressions

The staging of this wedding for pictures will be a creative journey I will thoroughly appreciate. Of course, dealing with the bride may be challenging. I have a gut feeling that there are skeletons in the closet that are just waiting to come out. I wish I weren't so skeptical by nature. Years of hanging around with colleagues in law enforcement shaped my perspective on situations. My need for perfection in everything I do stresses the equation. I'm letting it go. When I meet the bride-to-be tomorrow afternoon, I'll have a clearer vision, photographically and mentally, as to how to proceed. My purpose is to give lasting memories that stretch throughout the years, like the Wide-Angle lens, which I'll use to capture the gathering of family and friends.

I have a strange, heavy feeling about this event as I drive home. How could that be? The place is gorgeous, and it has so many possibilities. The interior is flawless, and the exterior is a work of art. The oversized gazebo, where the ceremony will take place, is magnificent. I can picture it on the wedding day, decorated with flowers and flowing organza lace fabric gathered around the columns that adorn it. The gazebo, more like an open-air room at a multi-million-dollar yacht club, will accommodate the guests beautifully and comfortably. It is screened all around with a light mesh that can be lowered should the need arise if the flying fiends of the marsh, also known as mosquitoes, decide to join the party. There is no obstruction to the pristine view of a tranquil lagoon that backs up to the property. Now, why do I feel this doom?

The Mon Cherie Coffee Shop is my favorite place to meet with the brides. It is central, non-assuming, comfortable, and has jaw-dropping pastries. So even if the brides-to-be are challenging, the chocolate goodies counteract the possible bitterness of the encounter. So far, she's about 20 minutes behind the scheduled meeting time. I don't know much about her; she may not be familiar with our town.

I was surprised when I received a call early this morning from Mrs. Fontaine, letting me know that Jane would be meeting me by herself. I could hear the hesitation and apologetic tone in her voice.

I didn't want to question it, but I felt uneasy. I couldn't understand why the bride would object to the groom's mother being present at the meeting when Mr. and Mrs. Fontaine were graciously covering the costs of the affair. Okay, wait and see. I'll be impartial and not judge her until I've met her. Somehow, I feel protective of this family. It may be because they're so genuinely kind to everybody, and that needs to be respected. I must shake this feeling off. I don't like myself; being defensive makes it challenging to be open and welcoming. Speaking of welcoming, she walks in while somebody holds the door open for her. She waltzes in and doesn't even acknowledge the person. I can see dealing with her may be a challenge, but for the sake of the Fontaines, I'll do my best and not fantasize about pushing her off the gazebo into the bayou waters after the ceremony.

Chapter 3

Camera Shy

"Good afternoon, Jane. Nice to meet you." I say, extending my hand in a friendly salute.

"Is this going to take long? I have a lot of things to do." Jane says without cracking the slightest smile.

"I will keep it as brief as possible. I must ask you some questions to ensure I capture everything you want for your special day."

"Fine, ask away. If it were up to me, we would elope and not have to deal with all the hoopla. But my future mother-in-law insists on making a big deal about it. Personally, I detest pictures.

"Even pictures that will keep your lasting memories of the occasion for years?"

"Sure, whatever; what do you need to know?"

"Do you have your dress picked out? Is it formal and elaborate, or classic lines with a modern flair? Do you have any pictures of it? That would give me an idea of what would be best suited for the background. You've seen the property, and it has a gorgeous backdrop for any setting. I want to make sure you're pleased with the outcome."

"I haven't given it much thought. You're the expert; I'm sure you'll know what to do. I don't want to spend much time posing for pictures. Especially pictures with people I'm only going to see one day in my life."

"I hope you and your future husband will see these people a lot. After all, you'll be part of a beautiful, caring family. If you're nervous, don't be. I met the Fontaines a while back at a charity event. Their friends and family members were all delightful. Walking into the event was like being drawn into a warm embrace."

"I'm not much for touchy, feely, but I'm sure I'll be fine. What else do you need to know?"

"If you have family or special friends, you may want unique pictures. Sometimes, these occasions lend themselves to making memories with those we don't see daily. But they're still very exceptional to us. It's a great way to reconnect."

"No," Jane says, breathing and rolling her eyes.

She doesn't want to talk about friends or family or the lack thereof. I'd better change the subject before I witness one of those run-out-of-the-room episodes Mrs. Fontaine mentioned.

"You are very photogenic, so I'm sure you will be a gorgeous, happy bride no matter what the locale or what you're wearing. Here is my card. Mrs. Fontaine has my information, but if you need to reach me or have any questions or concerns, please don't hesitate to call me. I won't keep you; I know you have to run.

And run, she does. I have never felt like such an inconvenience. She didn't even order anything to drink or eat. She doesn't know what she's missing. I will have a refill of my café au lait and order a chocolate éclair. I need a little sweetness after that encounter. What bride doesn't love pictures unless they have something to hide?

Chapter 4

Something's Up

"Come on, pick up the phone..."

"Hi Jessica, how did it go?"

"Renee, do you have a minute or two? I need to decompress from the meeting I just had."

"Sure, what happened this time? I'm glad I do what I do; dealing with the dearly departed is easier than dealing with the living." Renee chuckles.

"I told you I was meeting with the future Mrs. Ethan Fontaine. She is a strange one. Or perhaps she could be more interested in the wedding itself. The pictures, the decorations. It feels like she's just going through the motions but not really there."

"Maybe, just doing it to please her family."

"No, that's what is so bizarre. Jane doesn't have any family of her own, but she has the opportunity to be a part of the most loving, caring, and remarkable family in town. Who would not be excited about that? Not to mention, Ethan is well-educated, responsible, wealthy, and, not to point out the obvious, a handsome guy. Most women would be over the moon to be in her shoes. And yet, she is difficult and doesn't seem to value the dream wedding as an infinite gift."

"That doesn't make any sense. It's like being Cinderella, and when the prince places the glass slipper on her foot, she kicks him in the nose." Renee chuckles.

"I can just see that; thanks for making me laugh. I hope Ethan doesn't get kicked in the nose. There is something off about her. Maybe I can find something more before the wedding."

"Now, Jessica, I hate to say it. It is not your place to stick your nose, pardon the nose reference once again. And play sleuth. The Fontaines hired you as their photographer. You should not conduct a background check and utilize your past resources to learn more about this girl. The Fontaines are good businesspeople. They have security people working for them, as anyone with that kind of lifestyle has as a resource if need be. If there were something that stunk, they would have smelled it by now."

"You're just going to keep making nose references, right? You have a point; it is not my place to investigate the bride-to-be. I have to let it go. Going home and drawing a bath may wash away my apprehension."

"Would you like me to stop by your place after work? I'll bring a pizza, watch a mystery movie, and take our minds off our mystery-making.

"Sounds good, but I can't promise I won't bring Ms. Jane Doeth up in the conversation."

"Okay, I'll see you later. Must get back to work; the dead are waiting for me."

"Yes, that sounds comforting...The dead are waiting for you. See Ya."

Home sweet home, it is a welcome sight. Exiting the car and listening to the birds transports me to a peaceful oasis. It's time to run into the house; the mosquitoes are bloodthirsty and already have a couple of itchy bites. Usually, they're only super intrusive closer to sundown. And, of course, since I was not planning to go into the bayou, I didn't spray the necessary mosquito repellent. That was a mistake.

I may need a puppy and kitty repellent. Here are TK and TC jumping and rubbing against me. They're making it very difficult to walk, but they never fail to warm my heart.

I love my furry friends. I wouldn't want to come home without their loving exuberance.

"Okay, guys, first things first. Yes, I'm going to feed you. Are you guys hungry? It is a rhetorical question; the answer is always yes, no matter what time of day or night.

I'll draw the water in the tub while caring for the little ones. I don't know why that meeting with Jane was so draining. I may be reading too much into it. It could be wedding jitters or the stress of facing all these new people in her life, and not having a family foundation of her own may bring up unfounded fears. That's it. I'll relax and try my best not to read anything into it. Those psychology courses I took in the past can be relentless. Everything everyone does or says can lead to a forensic psychological profile. There is always a 'Why' backed up by a motive. Sometimes, it isn't fair to the people I meet. They don't know it, but before I realize it, they're under the magnifying glass, inspected and dissected.

Focusing on the present and what's most important. My furry friends ate; their freshwater bowls are full. I hear TC's soft purr and TK's delicate little growl. She tries to purr, but as we all know, dogs don't purr.

Now, that's more like it. The smell of lavender bath salts calms and relaxes me instantly. Of course, I also have a lavender candle. Can you overdo the lavender? I don't think so. But we'll know the answer if I fall asleep in the tub.

This can't be good. With my eyes closed, I take in the sauna experience, and the first thing I see is Jane. Jane, in her unsmiling face. The face that speaks volumes, which says--lady, why are you wasting my time with the picture nonsense?

I sink through the suds; that should eliminate that visual. But it's more than a graphic; it is a feeling I can't shake. Why is this feeling so intense?

After pizza, a movie, and great conversation, interlaced with Renee's humorous anecdotes, I can put all this to rest and get some rest tonight.

Chapter 5

True Confessions

"Pizza delivery! Hurry up, open the fortress, it's getting cold." Renee yells as she pounds on the door.

"I'm coming," I shout back as I unlock the three bolts on the door.

"This place is like Fort Knox; do you have enough locks on the door?"

"When you have unwelcome visitors in the middle of the night, and your world turns upside down, you become security conscious rather quickly."

"I don't blame you; better safe than sorry."

"Put the pizza down. I'll get the plates and the beverages. And push play, I have a new Agatha Christie for your viewing pleasure this evening."

"Sounds like the perfect evening, no drama for a change," Renee says, grabbing a slice and folding it as the right way to eat New York-style pizza.

"Now, there is an unwelcome sound," I say, reaching for the phone. I'm not in the mood to talk on the phone, especially since I don't recognize the number. It could be a prospective client, so I must answer.

"Hello! Hello!" I'm ready to hang up. Is that a whimper I hear? "Hello, is anybody there? Are you okay?"

"Hello, Jessica, this is Jane. I'm sorry to call you at home after hours, but I needed to speak with you." Jane speaks, her voice weak and unlike her voice from earlier in the day.

"Of course, not a problem. What can I do for you?"

"I need to apologize to you for my behavior earlier today."

"Oh, that is not necessary. Weddings can be stressful."

"No, I must apologize. I'm so sorry. I don't know how to act when people are nice to me. This whole thing with the Fontaines has made my emotions hit the roof. For so long, I've built a wall. After I lost my parents, I swore I would never let myself love again. It hurts too much. Then I met Ethan. He was just too perfect. I thought it would never last. So, I didn't have to worry about future developments."

I give Renee an apologetic look and pass a silent message that I must talk to this one.

"Go ahead, Jane. I'm listening," I say empathically.

"The way I acted today is not me. Actually, it is me. I and my way of not letting people get close to me. When I met the Fontaines, at Ethan's insistence, I was overwhelmed. I could never imagine being welcome into their home, family, and hearts. These people are the kindest, most generous, and most loving people I have ever met. I'm afraid I will wake up from a dream, and they will be gone.

When I meet people, I instinctively shut down. Act tough and keep people at arm's length. I don't trust anybody; I don't want to trust anybody. If I don't let them in, I don't have to face the pain of letting them go. So, now I'm in a place where I want to learn to trust again. I want to open my heart and learn to love again. To have a family and a marriage that goes beyond the fairytale." Her voice falters as if holding back tears. "You're part of the fairytale; I've seen beautiful pictures of weddings on your site. The way you capture the essence of love, not just from the groom and bride, but everyone at the event. That takes true talent. I'm so honored to have you photograph my wedding."

"Jane, it is my honor to be a part of such a fantastic occasion. Don't worry. Let's put this morning's jitters behind us and move forward to our next meeting. I would like to meet you at the Fontaine's, walk around the grounds, and get your input on where you see yourself and your groom. That way, the photo shoot can be short and sweet, and you both can enjoy your special day."

"Again, I'm sorry. I promise it won't happen again."

"Like I said, there is no need to apologize. Nerves can make anyone act a little weird from time to time. Don't give it a second thought. Call me tomorrow, and we'll pick a convenient date for all to do a walk-around, as they say. Have a good night."

"Good night, Jessica. Thank you for listening." Jane says as the line goes silent.

"What was that all about?" Renee asks as she reaches for her third piece of pizza.

How long was I on the phone? Glad Jane hung up, or there would be no pizza left. Before I get talking, I grab a piece.

"That was interesting. It was Jane, as you may have heard." I say, pausing to understand the emotionality behind Jane's words.

"Was she crying? I could hear a bit. Is the wedding still on?

"Yes, the wedding is still on, and from the sounds of it, it is better than ever. I totally misjudged Jane. She seemed so overbearing this morning. So rude in a way, so disinterested and cold about the whole event. Now, I understand. The poor girl has gone through so much. Since her parents were taken from her, she shut down. She built a wall to survive. To live and go through the motions of living without getting hurt. I can empathize with her." I say, as my watering eyes betray my stern demeanor.

"Well, it is good to know she's willing to open up and work towards enjoying the wedding and welcoming her new family," Renee says, reaching for another piece.

"Okay, let's watch the movie. Now, I look forward to a challenge-free wedding shoot."

Jane's renewed and humble attitude is going to turn the page on her fairytale wedding book."

Chapter 6

Wedding Day

The day has arrived, and I couldn't be more excited. I love being part of happy events where everybody's energy is ecstatic. Sure, there will be a few tears, but they'll be happy ones. I see the videographer is setting up his equipment. I've met Patrick McKnight before at different events; he always proves to be a real gentleman, a professional who's not unwilling to get his hands dirty or help others around him. He is a modern-day knight who upholds his family name.

This location is a pristine setting; I will capture the guests arriving with my 'Wide-angle' lens for a panoramic view, allowing me to obtain pictures of the scenery and the family and friends with such a gorgeous backdrop. Later, I will focus on the individuals in an impromptu and relaxed fashion before taking the traditional and expected photos of the main characters in this romantic affair.

"Hey, Jessica!" Patrick calls and waves to me to come over.

Going to him is easier since I only have the camera around my neck and my accessory bag in a cross-body pouch. He has a setup elaborate enough to film a motion picture. He is going all out; he has at least three cameras set up from different angles, aiming at the gazebo where the main event will occur. He is not going to miss a thing, that's for sure.

"Hi Patrick, nice to see you again. It's been a bit since we worked on an event together."

"It's always a pleasure working with you, Jessica. You always seem so calm in the face of chaos."

"I don't feel so calm on the inside. I want everything to be perfect, so the calm exterior is a false façade. But don't tell anyone. I have a feeling this one is going to be fun. The setting can't get any more beautiful, and the Fontaines can't be more accommodating."

"That is so true. The Fontaines invited me as a guest to the reception, and when I'm not filming, I can be eating. I'm sure they invited you also. I hope, or you'll think I'm their favorite new friend."

"Hate to blow your bubble; they invited me too. That's the kind of folks they are. In their eyes, there is a blurred line between people working for them and working with them. It feels good to be around them. I have to continue taking some atmosphere pictures. I'll buy you a drink at the reception."

"Not if I buy one for you first," Patrick laughs. He is such a charmer.

It's time to take my position by the altar behind the plant, placed strategically so I can capture everything and everyone, especially the procession down the aisle, without causing any distraction from the main characters. Of course, I'll be moving around once they're in place in front of the officiant, as I want to get as many angles as possible.

The show is starting. Mr. and Mrs. Fontaine walk regally to the front seats. Olivia (Mrs. Fontaine) spots me and waves. So glad this is not a covert operation, she would have compromised my location immediately. I wave back and smile. I am delighted to be here; this is more than an assignment. This assignment is an experience I'll never forget.

The groom and his two best friends walk casually down the aisle. They waive and laugh; they're having a genuinely fun time. I love informal weddings even though they're perfect and glamorous enough to adorn the pages of the most prestigious Bridal Magazines.

The bridal processional song commences, and my heart skips a beat as chills run up and down my spine. What is it about those notes that makes time stand still? I focus on the flowered archway that will frame the bride perfectly for a split second. I hold my breath, for this is the only time after she appears when she'll pause and then take her first step down the aisle towards her groom. Okay, where is she? I can only hold my breath for so long. Come on, cue the bride. Where is the wedding coordinator? I've known Francine for a long time. She's always on target. She directs her weddings with the charm of a Fairy Godmother and the precision of a drill sergeant. Something is wrong. Did the bride have a sneezing attack because of all of the flowers? Did she pass out due to the excitement?

I hate to leave my position and possibly miss the perfect shot, but there is something wrong with this picture.

Chapter 7

Breaking the News

Smiling as if there is absolutely nothing to be concerned with. I speed-walk towards the house, skirting the flowing fabric draped around the gazebo pillars and ensuring I don't end up in the water. I am not the most balanced person on high hills. That's why I always carry a pair of flats in my bag. Of course, at this point in the event, I thought I'd be safe wearing fancy shoes; boy, was I wrong.

As I round the corner into the back entrance of the house, with its open retractable glass wall, I crash into Francine. Her eyes are wide open, and panic is written all over her face.

"She's gone! She's gone." She whispers as we still support each other from our abrupt collision.

"Okay, take a breath. Let's go down the hall, where we can talk without the crowd's eyes. I want to know what's going on before everyone else panics."

"She's not in her room. Jane was sitting on the bench at the end of the bed, putting her shoes on. I left her to double-check and ensure everything was ready for her entrance. When I returned, she was gone, the veil was lying on the floor, the small table overturned, and one shoe left outside the French door. That's when I ran out to get you."

"Did you see anybody in the house who looked out of place?" I say, walking towards the room where Jane was to get ready.

"I didn't see anybody strange. The people setting up the wedding and the caterers are all people I have worked with on many occasions. They're like family.

"Maybe she just went out to get some air. She may have been feeling a bit overwhelmed. I've never been married, but I understand that's not unusual. I'm going to look around. You go and delay the proceedings. Grab Patrick and let him know what's happening, but don't let anybody overhear till we're sure she's gone. Just say my camera was acting up, and I needed another one from the car. Just ask them to--Bear with us. We want everything to be just right. And that's not a lie. Don't forget to smile."

Seeing white flowing fabric from behind a huge tree is a relief. Just as I thought, Jane needed to catch her breath and deal with the excitement. I'm running to make sure she is okay. I don't know what to say to her once I get there.

There is nothing to say. It was just a torn piece of Jane's wedding dress stuck to a low sapling branch. There were also a couple of sets of muddy footprints leading from the grass to the driveway and tire tracks that dug into a portion of the lawn. This doesn't look right. It's time to let everyone know the bride-to-be is missing. Ethan and everyone are going to be devastated. Did she leave on her own, had assistance, or was she kidnapped?

Chapter 8

Facing the Circumstances

Walking and thinking of how to break this to the family. What do you say when you don't know anything? How can I instill calmness when I'm panicking inside? My mind is working overtime. An image of the muddy footprints at the edge of the grass comes to mind. There are two different large but different sizes of muddy prints, unless we have a large male, judging from the depth of the imprint with two feet of various sizes. We may have two men carrying Jane into the vehicle. I don't recall seeing any high-heeled impression, so someone carried her away.

Glad to see Francine waiting at the door. I won't have to face the crowd alone.

"Did you see anything or anyone? I just stood there with a plastered smile, telling them to give us a minute; there was an issue with the gown. That's all I could think of at the time." Francine shares, rubbing her hands anxiously.

"You were not far off in your explanation about the gown. The gown seemed ripped and was missing along with the bride. Explaining this is not going to be easy."

As we step outside, the astute crowd must know something is wrong. All present turn and face us. The crowd's smiles slowly fade into shades of concern. They were expecting the bride; instead, they had the messengers of bad news.

"What's happening? Where is Jane? What's going on? Can I see her?" Ethan explodes with questions. His ashen face and moist eyes reveal his anguish.

"Ethan, there is no easy way to say this. We have to call the police. Jane is gone. It appears somebody took her." I try to explain without added emotion.

Ethan collapses to the ground and sobs. The crowd rises in unison and moves towards us as if a dam of emotions and uncertainty has breached. Peter, one of Ethan's best friends, appears by his side and helps him. He walks him into the house, with some of the crowd following behind. I must take control of the situation. I can't let anyone leave. Everyone here can be a witness; somebody must have seen something. There is no time to waste; I must call the police and contain the scene at the same time. Grabbing for my phone, I dial 911, raise my hand, and shout with as much authority as I can master. Nobody goes anywhere.

"911, what is your emergency?"

"My name is Jessica Martin. I'm at the Fontaine residence in Mandeville. I need to report a possible kidnapping."

"A kidnapping? Who, was kidnapped? And why do you assume it was a kidnapping?

"There are signs of foul play, and the missing person is the bride, Jane Doeth. You need to send the police as soon as possible. It's already been a bit since we realized she was missing. Time is of the essence. Please hurry."

"Maybe the gal got cold feet. It happens. There is no need to panic. The bride will show up as soon as she comes to her senses. Did you say Fontaines? Now, why in the world would somebody run away from marrying into the richest family in town?"

"Dispatch, I don't need your opinion on this or your conjecture. Send the police right away." I say with my no-nonsense voice.

"Yes, ma'am, I will send the troops." She says condescendingly as if my call was a significant inconvenience.

Chapter 9

It's Like Herding Kittens

Trying to control the masses is like herding kittens. Everybody is emotional and frightened. I gather my immediate, trusted friends and deputize them with my non-law-enforcement powers. Francine is at the ready.

"What do you need me to do?" She asks, almost standing at attention. This situation would be humorous if it weren't so serious.

"I need you and Patrick to spread the word to those you know and trust to contain the perimeter, as they say."

"Who's they?" Patrick asks with a smirk.

"They—as in police. No time for jokes right now." I say, suppressing my smile.

I hate to be so direct. But somebody has to take the lead.

I continue to say. "They must be your eyes, ears, and enforcers until the police arrive. Nobody leaves the premises.

We must have everybody accounted for until they get here. We have a sensitive matter in our hands. Some attendees are high-ranking luminaries who expect to be treated with the utmost respect and delicacy. But they need to remain here, nonetheless. Let's do it quickly before anybody decides to leave."

"I'll get on it," Francine says while tapping her headset and calling for Patrick. Technology can be our friend when time is of the essence.

The first plan of action is to question the kitchen staff. I see the open side door by the butler's pantry. It is conveniently located for the intake of deliveries just off the back of the driveway. Somebody must have heard or seen something.

Sometimes, the most minor details can be significant. Getting details before time fades memories is of the utmost importance.

"If I can have your attention, please," Trying not to shout but loud enough to be heard over the sound of pans and dishes in orchestrated discord. "I'm Jessica, and I need to ask you some questions. The police are on their way. By now, I'm sure you're all aware there has been an incident. Jane, the bride, is missing. Gathering any information that may be forgotten once the adrenaline leaves, and we're left with foggy minds, is important. Does anybody remember seeing anyone they didn't recognize who seemed out of place? Somebody lurking around?" I focus on Chef Henrie and his wife, Sous-Chef Marie, whom I've met and have a rapport with. Marie looks down immediately and wipes her hands on her apron frantically. What is that all about? I must get back to her. She has something to say, but maybe not in front of the rest.

I continue addressing the rest of the staff and the catering members hired for the event. "What were you doing, and where were you about half an hour ago? Were any of you standing or coming in or out of the side delivery entrance?" I say, looking around the room. Half a dozen people look at me with the look of a deer in headlights. There is absolutely no response from any of them.

"If anybody remembers anything or anyone, can you come and talk to me before the police get here? I will relay whatever you tell me to the officers. But we need to get as much information as soon as possible. I know they'll be asking the same questions, but if we have something tangible to share, they may be able to expedite matters and find Jane sooner rather than later. Anyone? Please think about what you were doing. Where were you standing? Did you go out the side door for a cigarette, and did you observe someone arriving late? Parking a truck in an odd position. Hearing any scuffle or muffled sounds? Anything, anything at all?"

There is something odd about this. Being around investigators, I've learned that nothing means something. The lack of cooperation or coming forward with any information speaks volumes. It's up to me to turn the pages.

Wow, this is going to be a tough one for the detectives. Do these people not want to cooperate, or do they think we'll talk to the real cops when we have to? Having a badge makes an impact. People only want to come forward nowadays and implicate themselves if they absolutely have to. I'll circle back to the chefs after I touch base with Francine and Patrick to see how they keep the guests from a mass exodus. I'm sure everyone here is shocked but wants to cooperate to see the safe return of the bride-to-be, who at this point remains a bride-to-be. We are so close, and we don't know how far.

Next, I'm going to the main room to see how Ethan and his parents are doing. At least I can be there for comfort and support before the police arrive. This will be a long day, and not in the happy way it was supposed to be.

Chapter 10

The Troops Have Arrived

Two vehicles pull up in the driveway, a black and white Mandeville Police SUV and a shiny black unmarked SUV from which two suits appear. Obviously, the detectives are here. The dispatcher must have emphasized the word kidnapping, even though she seemed dismissive.

It is interesting how they arrive with no lights or sirens. Does that mean they're not in a hurry to locate the missing person? Have they given up before they begin? What's happening right now? People here in Louisiana seem to work in a different time dimension. But, come on, people show some urgency in the matter. I'll meet the detectives outside. The guests, except for sipping their cocktails, are frozen in time. That is to be expected. They need to calm their nerves in such an unforeseen situation. Hopefully, not too many sips before talking to the detectives and ending up with a bunch of incoherent nonsense.

"Detectives, I presume. I'm Jessica Martin. I made the 911 call. Please come in.

"You presume, correctly. I'm Detective Watson, Elliot Watson, and this is my partner, Detective Scott Holden." One speaks, and the other nods as they walk in, looking around as if taking inventory of the place.

"A couple of my friends and associates and I ensured nobody left the premises. I figure you may want to question everybody who was here at the time of the disappearance." I say, trying to sound calm and collected, unlike how I feel.

"That's Good thinking. We'll go in and introduce ourselves and reassure everybody we're on the job. The units outside will look around for any obvious evidence, so it stays contained. After we make the necessary introductions, starting with Mr. and Mrs. Fontaine, we'd like to speak with you and get details of what may have occurred."

"You know Mr. and Mrs. Fontaine?"

"Oh yes, the Fontaines are well known and respected by our department. They're good people; this is a regrettable circumstance, and we'll do everything we can to find out what happened and bring the girl back."

"Ladies and gentlemen, we're with the Mandeville Police Department. I'm Detective Watson, and this is my partner, Detective Holden. We will do our best to gather as much information as possible as soon as possible so we can reunite the bride with her fiancé and family. We don't have any definite leads as to what happened at this time, but I promise we'll do our best to get things rolling."

"This is taking too long already. I came for a wedding, and there was no wedding. I have to get back to Miami. I have a business to take care of." A loud and slightly slurred voice is heard from the back of the room, drawing the attention of all present.

"Perhaps you would like to be the first to answer our questions," the Detective says, moving in the direction of the voice and waving his hand in a come-along manner.

"Sure, let's get this over with. I should have known not to come. If it weren't for my wife insisting, I would have happily stayed home. I don't even know these people. I told you I didn't want to bother with this." He says, looking back at the mortified lady, hiding her face and trying to fade into the wall.

So why did they come? What is the connection between the Fontaines, this charismatic individual, and his classically beautiful and well-dressed lady? Talk about an odd couple. Now, there is a mystery.

Chapter 11

Not Waiting For Answers

While the detectives take charge of the guests in the central area and conduct interviews with the crowd, I will sneak to the kitchen and see if I can speak to Marie privately.

"Where do you think you're going?" An unfamiliar voice propels itself from behind me. As I turn, I see a very young, uniformed officer by his stance and hand hovering over his sidearm. This may be his first assignment, fresh out of the academy. His shaking right hand, slightly touching his gun, is not a threatening gesture; it's more like checking to make sure it's there and not left behind in his locker.

"I was just going to the kitchen to get some water; I need to take something for my headache, officer," I say with my most disarming smile. "Is that OK, officer?" Emphasizing the word officer does the trick. He waves in the direction

I was going in and, in his best stern voice, tells me to get back to the main group where the detectives are, as soon as I get my water.

"Yes, officer, of course." A salute is fitting, but I restrain myself.

Now to find Marie and talk to her before Officer "Newbie" sends SWAT after me...

"Hi, Marie. Could I speak with you for a minute?" I call out as she leans on the door frame facing the driveway.

"Yes, of course, Jessica. What do you need?" she says as she again starts rubbing her clean hands on her apron. That seems to be her "tell," the go-to motion she automatically does when nervous or apprehensive.

"Did you see anything that you want to tell me about? I know you saw or heard something, but why don't you want to tell me about it?"

"I'm afraid one of them saw me. I don't know what to do. The guy put his finger to his lips, like not to say anything, and then he motioned, cutting the throat and pointing at me. It was a clear sign that if I said anything, they would kill me. I told Henrie, and he told me to keep quiet and mind my business."

"I can understand your hesitation, but with all these people, how would they know you're the only one who saw them. We need to help the police as best we can to get Jane back safely."

"That's the thing, even though one guy was carrying her, it didn't appear she was struggling."

"Well, maybe they sedated her. You need to talk to the detectives and tell them everything you just told me. You owe it to the Fontaines; they're good people, and we need to help in every way possible.

"OK, I will talk to the detectives. Will you stay with me?"

"I will walk with you. I don't know the protocol for interviewing witnesses, but I promise I won't be far."

There is an eerie feeling throughout the house. Now, many more plain-clothed officers are sitting with guests at the individual tables set up for the reception. The reception area in the main ballroom of the house has transformed from a festive, glamorous, romantic, and inviting environment to a war room for interrogation. The disconnection is surreal but, unfortunately, very real.

At the oversized, edged glass double-French door entrance to the main room, officer "Newbie" stands almost at attention. Lucky me!

"Officer, thank you for letting me through to the kitchen earlier. May I ask your name? I don't see your nameplate on your uniform."

"I left it in my locker. My name is Sandoval, Officer Sandoval." The officer says, looking down at his shoes, unsure if he's embarrassed or just checking that he didn't leave his working boots behind.

"It's good to meet you officially, Officer Sandoval. We need to speak to Detective Watson; Marie needs to speak to him. It's time sensitive." I say as charmingly and respectfully as possible to ensure he acts immediately.

Hesitantly, he reaches for the doorknob, unaware of his procedure, when he interrupts a detective to bring forth pertinent information. It is torture to see a young man so uncertain, but we all have been there, rookies at our jobs, until the years of experience take over, and there is no occasion for hesitation.

Chapter 12

Something Doesn't Fit

No sooner than Officer Sandoval gives the Detective the message, the Detective concludes the questioning with the man sitting at his table. Watson motions for Marie to join him. He courteously slightly rises from his chair as she sits. I can tell he detects her uneasiness. Marie looks at me as a child seeking comfort from their mom. I wish I could hold her hand and assure her everything would be alright. All I can offer is my reassuring smile, a wink, and a thumbs-up. She smiles, takes a deep breath, and starts talking to Detective Watson. That's my signal to step outside and wait my turn to speak to the detectives. I wish I had more to offer in terms of information. As the adrenaline dissipates, I feel listless and ready to nap.

I'll retrieve and secure my camera and equipment. I don't think I will be taking any more pictures today. Pictures! That's what I need to do. I need to look at the photos of the guests coming and going before the ceremony. After all, you never know what a wide-angle lens will capture that the eye dismissed.

Suddenly, my grogginess has disappeared, and I almost run towards my camera with renewed exuberance. It's time to change into my flats; this running in high heels is not cutting it.

Having my camera bag gives me a strange sense of creation and adventure. It's like an unforeseen force that guides me to know I'll find something. There must be something or someone who stands out or tries too hard to blend in. If somebody in these pictures doesn't belong, I'll find them.

Yes, this is the perfect spot to immerse myself in reviewing the pictures. I am so grateful for digital photography, which allows me to view the images within seconds of taking them. I'll tether the camera to my tablet, see the pictures in detail, and enlarge them so I don't miss a thing.

I better tell the officer guarding the interrogation ballroom where I'd be if the detectives need to speak with me.

"Officer Sandoval, could you do me a favor?"

"Well, that depends..." He says, seeming much more relaxed and almost cracking a smile.

"Could you please let Detective Holden or Detective Watson know I'll be in the library if they need me? I say, in disbelief, that sentence sounds like the beginning of a game of "Clue."

"Miss Jessica Martin will be in the library...hopefully, not holding a candlestick..." He says, chuckling to himself.

"I don't believe I gave you, my name."

"I have ways to find things out; after all, I am a cop."

"And an astute one at that. Thank you, Officer Sandoval." I say and start walking away before this conversation unnecessarily lingers. What's happening to this guy? One minute, he's shy and awkward; the next, he's confident and almost congenial. Oh well, there is a mystery for another day. Now, I must concentrate on what evidence, if any, is in the pictures I took.

My eyes burn as I scan each frame intently. I am still determining what or who I'm looking for, but I'll know when I find it. There has to be something that's going to lead us somewhere. Is there a knock on the door, or am I hearing things? This library is so soundproof, it's like a tomb for the tomes.

"Jessica, are you in there? May I come in?" Marie speaks in a hushed voice as if respecting library decorum.

"Yes, please come in."

"I brought you tea and finger sandwiches. You must be famished."

"I haven't thought about food, but now that I see those cute tiny sandwiches, I could eat. Thank you so much. How did you know I was here?"

"The young officer guarding the interview room told me you were here. He asked me to bring you something to eat. I think fancies you, as they used to say..." Marie says with a wink.

"Where there is mystery, there must be romance. It's funny; I'm old enough to be--well, his older sister. It's better to be liked than not."

"Did you find anything yet?" Marie says, peeking over my shoulder.

"Not yet, but my gut says to keep going. Maybe it was just hunger, but my gut is on a mission now that I've eaten some delicious sandwiches. I'd better get back to it. Thank you, Marie, for bringing this."

"Don't thank me, thank Officer Dreamy." She chuckles as she walks toward the door."

"You, thank him, for me. A simple thank you, don't add anything to it." I half-whisper back to her and return to the self-imposed assignment.

Chapter 13

Red Shirt and Khakis

Who's this guy? I ask as if I would hear an answer by saying it out loud. There he is again. Not really dressed for the occasion. He does stand out with his red polo shirt and khakis. Is it Jake from State Farm? I must see where else he appears. He is definitely not trying to blend in. The catering people were all on the other side of the mansion, and even though it was sweltering and humid, they were all wearing black uniforms. So, who is he, and why is he here?

In this picture, he is waving and a bit blurry, as if he is moving fast toward something or someone. Very interesting. He grabs Ethan's arm, and in the next frame, Ethan shrugs him off and moves toward the back of the house. I must speak with Ethan.

I bolt out of the library as if I'm on fire; in a way, I am. I need to know who this guy in red is and his connection with Ethan.

I spot a couple leaving by the front door. People are allowed to go after the preliminary interview. Escorting them out, I see Anne Acosta, the charming house manager. She's too kind and good at what she does to be addressed as a maid—she's so much more.

"Anne, do you have a minute?"

"For you, Miss Jessica, I make time."

"Have you seen Ethan or know where he is?"

"Yes, I just brought him something, but he won't eat. He is so upset. Poor thing. He is in his room. Come with me, I'll take you to him."

"Thank you. I must speak with Ethan right away." I say as I stay in stride with this dynamo of a lady. She can move.

"Ethan, honey, can we come in? I have Miss Jessica with me," she says after knocking with a unique little sequence of tapping. She's been around since Ethan was little, so I'm sure they have their special code.

"Sure, come in." He answers, sounding like life has been sapped from his soul.

"Ethan, I don't want to intrude. I can't imagine what you're going through. But I know everybody is doing their best to find Jane and bring her back to you." I say to him as he stands motionless, looking out at the lagoon's panoramic view from his picture window.

He clears his throat and raises his hands to his face. I hear him taking a deep breath, straightening his shoulders, and turning to face me.

"Jessica, what can I do for you?" He says this as if this is a professional meeting without any emotionality.

I get directly to the point. "Ethan, I have been reviewing the pictures I took as the guests arrived. In one of the photos, there is a man wearing a red polo shirt and khakis. He approached you, and you shrugged him off and walked away. Who is he?

"He is nobody; he was just talking nonsense and trying to stir trouble between Jane and me."

"What do you mean? Do you know him?" I know he's not in the sharing mood, but this guy could be crucial to today's events. I have to push him for information, no matter Ethan's discomfort.

"He said Jane wasn't who I thought she was. She was a scam artist, and I needed to call the wedding off. He said if I didn't, we would all be sorry."

"So, he practically threatened you, and you didn't share this with the police? This is not the time to feel sorry for yourself; go to bed and put the covers over your head. If you love this woman, you will grab one of the detectives and tell them about this guy."

"I think he was just an ex with an axe to grind and making trouble for Jane and me."

"He accomplished that, didn't he? Jane has been kid-napped; the wedding is off. I think he did an outstanding job causing trouble. Now, we need to find him and find out exactly what part he played in the kidnapping."

"I don't really know who he is, other than he said he dated her for a time, till she tried to extort money from his parents. He said his name was Lee or Leon, or something like that. I know Jane, she's not like that. I told him to get off my property, or I would have security take care of him."

That's it, you have more information than you know. You're coming with me and talking to the detectives." I say, grabbing his hand and pulling him out of his cocoon of a room.

Chapter 14

Person of Interest

Officer Sandoval's observation skills are growing with leaps and bounds. He sees Ethan and me speed-walking down the hall, and he intuitively opens the door and waves us into what we're calling the interrogation room. I cannot hold myself in check. We approach the table, and I tell the Detective we must speak with him now. Detective Watson looks up from his notes with a furrowed brow. His expression changes immediately upon seeing the groom, still held hostage by my hand around his arm, as if brought to him unwillingly. He brings a slight smile to his lips so as not to seem rude to the lady he is speaking to, and he tells her she's good to go. He hands her his card and tells her that if anything she remembers or any other information comes up, don't hesitate to call him.

I give her the purse she had placed on the table to speed up her exit. After all, every minute counts.

Detective Watson, Ethan, spoke to a person of interest who stood out in the photographs I took. This person threatened him and his family. There is little to go on, but he has a possible name: Lee or Leon. If we scan the outdoor cameras, we can see what car he arrived in and, from the right angle, get a plate. We need to act fast. I'm sure he has something to do with why Jane is gone.

"OK, Ms. Martin, slow down a bit. Last I checked, I was still the lead Detective on this case, along with my partner, diligently conducting interviews and obtaining pertinent information. I appreciate your enthusiasm, but I'm sure we can handle this."

That's right. This is New Orleans, where, to some, the little ladies still don't need to be super assertive. It's time to change my approach.

"Detective Watson, you must excuse me. I know you're a seasoned professional, and your partner, Detective Holden, is the best. I am excited to bring some information that may aid in your efforts to get Jane back. I'll sit here quietly if Ethan overlooks some details from what he shared with me a few minutes ago. Would that be alright?"

"Yes, I assume that will be fine." With a look that says, don't let me regret this.

"Thank you, kindly," I say, sitting demurely and moving the chair for Ethan next to me as I nudge him to start talking.

"Miss Martin, could you get me copies of the photographs with this individual?"

"Yes, I just need to go back to the library. There is a printer there I can use to get some prints done right away. And Detective, it's Jessica."

"After you get the prints, meet me in the security office, I believe it's over the garage. You can point them toward where this individual may have come from since you know where you were when you took the pictures."

"Great idea, that's what I call teamwork. I'll be right there." Curbing my enthusiasm, something about being around law enforcement scenarios ignites something in me. It is the puzzle-making mystery that mystifies me. And, of course, finding the bride.

There is something about what this Lee or Leon character said about Jane being a scam artist. What if there were some facts about the allegation? That is something I'm going to have to look into. Well, my newfound team, Detective Watson, and his trusty partner, Detective Holden. They don't know it yet, but we're working together.

Isn't this cozy in a technical, covert NASA launch type of setup? We start with a bolt-like metal door that closes silently and locks automatically behind us. This security outpost is state-of-the-art , and if I'm correct, the width of the window glass signifies it is bulletproof. It is interesting to see little mini windows with latches at different heights. They look like bank teller windows, but what may pass through them may not be currency exchange but firepower. I hope they never need to use it. I want to visualize the little ports used as bird feeders from time to time. Twenty screens encompass the entire property; another set of ten screens to the side cover the area a mile or two down the main road and entrance to the driveway. Now, I'm so impressed that I'm speechless.

"Miss Martin, Jessica," Detective Watson says with a smile. "Let me introduce you to Stephan. He is the head of the security team for the Fontaine family."

"It's nice to meet you," I say, not seeming intimidated by his large and muscular frame.

"Have a seat over here. The stool rolls so you can direct and point to which screen may be best for viewing in relation to the photographs you took. May I have the photos, so we know what or who we're looking for?" He seems friendly, but I wouldn't want to be his adversary.

Stephan means business. He rolls up his sleeves and starts giving tactical commands.

"Jim, roll the video to one hour before anybody arrives," he says, directing his attention to screen one.

Detective Watson is standing back from the monitors, drinking his coffee, and reading over his notes. He seems unattached to this part of the action, but I'm sure he is working overtime in his mind.

I'm getting impatient. This part of the investigation could take a while, but we don't have a choice. It's one of those things that, even though it's time-consuming, is necessary to ensure you get all the details. For the first hour, there is nothing of significance. Most cars drive up to the circular driveway, hand their keys to the valet, and walk into the house's main entrance.

I look at the photo's timestamp and bring that to Stephan's attention.

"How about we double back from when the subject first appears on the frame and see if we can track him back to where he parked? He did not follow suit and drive his car to the valet; we can be certain of that," I say, trying not to sound impatient or commanding.

"I like that," Stephan says without hesitation. "OK, Jim, you heard the lady, advance to this time on the photo, and then slow mode back from there."

I did not anticipate such cooperation, but I like it. My team is coming together just fine.

"There he is!" Shouts Jim with unexpected exuberance.

We find ourselves hovering over Jim without any thought to personal space. We have all come together for a common purpose: to find out who this guy is and bring back the bride. This close-net mission just made us family.

Chapter 15

On The Look Out

Finding this elusive intruder propels Detective Watson into the front row of screen viewers. Jim is moving at lightning speed over the keyboard. The images move back and forth seamlessly, searching from the time of contact with Ethan, which I captured on the still camera, and then moving back, tracing his steps to where he immerses himself in the scene.

It is not difficult to spot the man in the red polo shirt until he disappears behind the oversized live oak tree with its low-hanging branches and wide trunk. This tree blocks the line of vision. Nobody blinks as we watch the screen. The room explodes with excitement as a car emerges and drives down the road seconds after our subject disappears from view.

"We got him!" Stephan says, restraining in his exuberance. "Stop-frame, back it up, and enlarge before the sun's glare hits the window."

We're holding our breath to see what develops next.

The images are scanned frame by frame. The side of the vehicle gives us the make, model, and color. Nothing gets past the detective, who states with renewed vitality. That's a silver 2019 or 2020 Ford Fusion SE; they stopped making them in 2020. Can you enlarge the back window view any further? He asks, tapping Jim's shoulder.

"This is as large as I can get without further enhancement. What exactly are you looking for?"

"That's a rental car. Can you see the barcodes on the back window? Rental cars have GPS, so we can track them and know their origin and destination. But we have to act fast."

"Detective! Jim calls out. This image is a front view from the camera tracking the outgoing traffic from the property. There is our guy, with his easy-to-spot "me" red shirt. And one more thing."

"What is it?" About three or four of us say in unison.

"On the dash, there is what appears to be a parking sticker with the number 49 and the green Enterprise logo." Jim shares it proudly.

"My work is cut out for me. I'm going to the library and setting up shop for a bit. I must call the rental company before this guy returns the vehicle and disappears." Detective says.

"Detective Watson, is there anything I can do?"

"Not that I can think of. You've been most helpful. I really appreciate it." He says, actually smiling.

For some reason, I feel empty. There must be something more I can do. Unlike a TV show, this doesn't get wrapped up in an hour.

I'll go to the library and clear my equipment so the detectives can be comfortable during the investigation.

I'm sure the second wave of law enforcement personnel will arrive soon. They'll set up phone recording and monitoring equipment in case of a ransom demand. At this point, we don't know for sure if it is a kidnapping, but we have to be open to all scenarios.

Before I go, I must see how the Fontaines are doing. I can't leave without letting them know how I feel and that I'm there for them, whatever they need.

It's time to go home and research who this guy is and the connection to Jane. I'll keep tabs on the detective and hope he may share some information when he attains it. The trick is to get myself in the circle of trust without being ousted for interfering with an ongoing investigation. So far, it has been going well. I brought to light something valuable in their pursuit of finding the individual who may be the main suspect. I need to be in the loop. Once I know the subject's full name, I can start pounding the cyber pavement. I'll start with Social Media and every other source that can bring a happy ending to a dismal beginning."

I have a face, but I don't have a name. Fortunately, I know someone who may help me with it. Is it wrong to utilize my resources? I could wait until the detectives on the case and any technical limitations are revealed with their facial recognition. Or, I can call and get assistance from the top law enforcement connection, the FBI. I am conflicted; I'm not officially working on the case. And I am not law enforcement myself anymore. But time is of the essence. A life can be in danger. There is no time to wait. I'll make a call now; if need be, I'll face the consequences later.

"Hi Robert, you answer so quickly, you startle me," I say, chuckling to soften the blow of my request.

"You startle? That would be a first. How are you?

"I'm good, but I have a situation," I say hesitantly.

"Ok, I take it this is not a social call. Are you in trouble? I'll fly down."

"No, I'm not in trouble, but trouble is afoot. You know the photo assignment I had for Fontaine's wedding I was telling you about—well, the bride is missing. We're assuming, by the looks of it, she was kidnapped."

"Kidnapped? Has it been twenty-four hours since she went missing or got taken?

"No, not yet. It happened this morning. It's been a long day; it seems like a week since it happened. There have been so many discoveries, interviews, and, well, you know, the routine. Add the fact that it takes place at a mansion before a wedding. It was chaos."

"I'm sure the local authorities have already alerted the Feds, and they should be taking the lead on this. I could make some calls and find out who will be the lead agent on this case. I know how you are; you will insert yourself in the investigation somehow," Robert says, letting out an audible breath.

"I already did. I had taken pictures of the guest coming in, and after examining the photos, we found that we had a person of interest. We may have a first name, but that's all. I want to know who this guy is and his connection with Jane before it's too late. I need your facial recognition software to get an ID. Pronto!"

"I could tell you to wait until the local FBI gets there and they start the process, but you want to get ahead of red tape and help the family. I understand. For the sake of urgency, since we don't know how dangerous these perps are, email me the best shots you have. I'll see what I can do. I'll head out to the office now and get the process going. I'll also call NOLA's FBI headquarters and let them know in the nicest way I can that you have information they can use."

"Thank you so much. Nobody deserves to be taken at any time, and we know that happens much too often, but on their wedding day. That goes beyond words."

"Oh, what more thing...how do you manage to be in the middle of crime no matter the occasion?"

"Lucky, I guess, as I always have the resolve to make things right. Maybe it's my calling." I say, hanging up.

Chapter 16

Illusive Intruder

I bolt upright as the ringer on my cell phone shatters my dreams, and I'm forced to face reality. I reach for the phone, not out of curiosity but because I need to stop the annoying sound. As my heart slows down, I can pick up the phone and clear my throat. As I glance at the time before clicking the answer button, my annoyance returns when I see it's only 6:30 a.m. on Sunday.

"Hi Robert," I say, sounding cheery despite my grogginess.

"I woke you, didn't I? I was in a hurry to share the information I've obtained.

"This information must be earth-shattering. What is it over there? 4:30 in the morning. Do you ever sleep?"

"Only on a need-to basis," he says, chuckling. "Now, do you want to hear the news, or should I call later after you have coffee?" He asks mockingly.

"I can smell it brewing on my way to get my cup. Now, tell me what you have."

"We have intel on our elusive intruder—it wasn't too difficult."

"He is a criminal, so he was on your database; I knew it..." I say, without yelling, Aha! "Actually, he is not a criminal; his name is Jason Lee, from a well-established Korean American family. He has top security clearance from the government. Jason is a highly skilled Senior Forensic Accountant who works for some of the most prestigious financial institutions in the world. He has assisted the FBI and other law enforcement agencies with cases where somebody needed his expertise.

"Just because in his professional life he is a hero, doesn't mean he is not an obsessed and dangerous predator on the personal side. What was he doing there? We need to know, and we need to know now."

"I spoke to Special Agent Larson, who is in charge of this case at the NOLA headquarters. Lora Larson is her full name. She's very forthcoming and open to collaboration, as long as people are assets and not liabilities in her investigation."

"Will she be open to having me as a collaborator? Would you know?"

"I already opened the door for you. I've worked with Lora several times and told her about your involvement and assistance in this case. I told her you were the one who spotted the questionable individual at the wedding and brought it to the attention of the detectives. She would like you to come down to the headquarters and bring all the pictures in which this individual shows up."

"Will this set well with the NOLA police detectives? I don't like getting caught in the middle of law enforcement conflicts."

"Don't worry about that. Larson will take care of smoothing any feathers that may get ruffled; she's all about expediting the process and recovery of the package, in this case, the bride-to-be. She's excellent at what she does," he says with a little too much enthusiasm, if you ask me.

"How about our suspect, subject, whatever we want to call him. Have they found him yet?" I say, getting back to the business at hand.

"They located him at the La Fitte Hotel in the French Quarter. It was easy with all the rental car information the detectives shared. It's not like he was hiding or trying to be incognito.

"Do you know if the local police made contact with him already?"

"I'm sure the Feds will take point on this, since it has all the markings of a kidnapping. Just leave it up to Larson; she'll handle it."

"You have a lot of confidence in Larson, is she that good?" I say, trying to keep sarcasm out of my voice.

"She's highly skilled and a professional. I've enjoyed working with her on a few cases." Robert is just stating the facts.

"I still think he was there under nefarious pretenses. In other words, up to no good." I say, changing the subject. Too much flattery before coffee.

"What is the number one rule in investigations? Be impartial until you have all the evidence. We've discussed this before."

"Yes, we have, but I still have a gut feeling he is up to something. I'm on my way. Bye!" I say before he has another chance to shoot my theory down.

Chapter 17

Meeting The Feds

When I drove Leon C Simon Boulevard in the past, I never realized that this Federal Building was fenced all the way around. Am I going to face a challenge just getting in? I'm glad I threw on a blazer; maybe I'll blend in, and they'll let me through the gates.

As I approach the guard, I smile—just a little. We don't want to be over the top. People approaching federal buildings are not known to be giddy. If you're there, you must be there for serious business. That's not me, but sometimes we must play a part.

"The guard asks with a big, bright smile, "Good morning. Are you here to see anyone in particular?" He didn't get the memo that only serious business is conducted on these premises."

"I'm Jessica Martin, here to see Special Agent Lora Larson," I say as I prepare to provide my ID.

I look up and see the gate opening.

As he says, "Ms. Martin, they're expecting you. On the second floor to the right, you'll find the conference room.

Well, that was easy. Robert did put in a good word for me. Now, it's my turn to present an air of composure, knowledge, and helpfulness without seeming too eager and acting out of place. Of course, the thought of Robert working with Agent Larson has spiraled me a bit. I keep telling myself that Robert and I will always be friends, nothing more or less. What he does on his time is his business—there is no reason why I should be suspicious or curious. So, why am I bothered by it? I'll ponder that another day.

The elevator door suddenly opens—much too soon, on the second floor, and a striking and statuesque blonde creature in a designer-looking fitted pantsuit greets me.

Her hand is outstretched, ready to shake, and her pearly smile is right out of a toothpaste commercial.

I instantly compose myself and shake the deer in the headlights of my face. I shake hands, and I stutter as I introduce myself.

"No need, I know who you are, Jessica; Rob told me all about you and how your gift for focusing on details can be a great asset in this investigation. I'm looking forward to hearing what you have to share with us."

I hope her confidence is contagious, as I've never felt this vulnerable before. I must concentrate on the case at hand. There is a life at stake. Time to step up my game, be me, and forget about what may be or have been between this person and Robert. She called him "Rob," but he doesn't let anybody call him "Rob." What's up with that? A little too familiar if you ask me. I must get out of my head as I enter the conference room occupied by several agents.

I take a deep breath as I place the folder with the still photos on the conference table and hand over the flash drive to Special Agent Larson. She makes brief introductions of the agents present and lets them know I may have pertinent information about the case. The agents settle into their seats, eyes on me. I retrieve a flash drive from my bag and hand it to a tech agent, who quickly connects it to a large monitor at the front of the room.

"These are shots from the morning of the wedding," I begin. "Special Agent Hunt has identified this man, but I still have questions."

An image fills the screen: the accountant, standing near the back of the venue, partially hidden by a decorative column.

Special Agent Larson nods. "Yes, Hunt briefed me. The accountant with top clearance, aiding law enforcement, staying at the La Fitte Hotel. His name is Jason Lee. He is a Senior Forensic Accountant. We need to know what his connection with this family is or with the perpetrators. I'm curious as to how he fits in this situation.

The agent clicks through several shots showing him in different positions. "He wasn't mingling. He was observing. That stands out to me."

"Agreed," Larson says. "But let's not jump to conclusions. Any other details?"

I hesitate, as I approach the agent with the clicker. "May I?" I say, as I motion for him to hand it over, after all, I know what we're looking for, and we don't have all day. "We also caught him on the security cameras leaving the wedding venue just before Jane disappeared. That's how we got the car's make and model and all the pertinent details that led us to him."

Larson's brows lift. "Show me."

I display the photo of him walking away. I switch the file to the security video, then fast forward to the car leaving the gates.

"That gives us a lot to explore," Larson says. "We know who he is, and he can't deny being there. Now we need to find out why he was there and how he's involved in the alleged kidnapping."

"What is his connection to the bride-to-be?" I add. "I showed the pictures to Ethan, the groom, and his parents. No one at the wedding party recognized him."

Larson leans in. "I take it the local PD and the detectives are aware of this individual."

Trying not to sound unaware of the costumery logistics, I say, "I was expecting the main detectives on the case to join us this morning."

Larson chuckles to herself as she says, "That's not how things work with different agencies. You got extra points because you went outside protocol, contacted your 'special agent', and shared the pictures. Right now, we have a lot more information to go on than the locals. We will share this information in due course."

"I see," I say, even though I'm confused about how the hierarchy plays when a life may be at stake. "Let's hope he is still in town so we can question him and find the motive for his lurking around at a wedding, uninvited."

"We?" Larson asks, raising an eyebrow.

"I meant you, the Special Agents in charge. I get a little overzealous when people may be in danger and throw protocol or competition out the window."

Larson's tone softens. "Your instincts are sharp. Let's find out why our 'hero accountant' was there."

I nod, determination in my eyes. "Let's hope we're not too late, and he has left town."

"No worries, we have eyes on him, since Rob shared the ID of the subject. So far, he's staying put." Interjects a young and exuberant agent. He introduces himself on the run as he pulls his phone out of his jacket. Turning halfway back, he says, "I'm Agent Clark." And proceeds ahead towards the stairs.

As we reach the parking lot, I assume this is the end of my collaboration. I head over to my car and let them do their job. I feel a bit down. I would like to have more to say or do. I'm not one for setting things out and letting others do the work. After all, rumor has it, I have a keen eye for details.

"Hey Jessica! Larson shouts. "It would be easier if you drove with us, you can get your car later. I assure you it will be safe."

"Yes, of course, just grabbing my phone--be right there," I shout back, pleased that Special Agent Lora Larson seems to be accepting of my help, but I'm not letting my guard down.

Chapter 18

If The Walls Could Talk

A rriving at La Fitte Hotel to question a person of interest during daylight hours seems so out of place. We are on a mission, and time is of the essence. This scene contrasts with the evening flavor of this locale. It is nestled on the corner of Bourbon Street, it exudes timeless charm, its wrought-iron balconies are draped with hanging ferns, and there is the perpetual hum of jazz music. The dimly lit interior is thick with the scent of aged wood and secrets, as the walls hold stories of a bygone era. In my evening visits to this hotel, I felt history and mystery dance together in the flickering candlelight. We are here for a different type of mystery. Hopefully, these walls will help reveal the truth.

I am jolted from my reverie by the sudden stop of the Jeep Chief Wagoneer L; we're riding as we abruptly pull up to the place. I've always wondered if the FBI and other authorities drive such covert vehicles equipped with functional police lights, all black with tinted windows to maintain a low profile during operations and interviews. Why do they arrive at the places so swiftly that it draws undue attention from any passerby who happens to be in the vicinity?

Maybe I'll ask Robert that question. I'm not on such friendly terms with Agent Larson at this time. And I don't want to get off on the wrong foot since she allowed me to come along on this interview and wouldn't want to come across disrespectfully. It's too soon for her to understand my sarcastic, funny take on things.

Larson, another unnamed agent, and I are walking towards the elevator as it has already been ascertained that the subject is staying on the third floor. I feel introductions should be made, but when you're standing indoors with a man over six feet four, with a black suit, white shirt, and dark sunglasses, who seems to exude I'm on the job, don't talk to me. There is no way I will be the one to exchange pleasantries. I'm sure sooner or later, he'll be addressed at least by last name, and I'll commit it to memory. Of course, Agent Clark, who introduced himself earlier as he flew by, has already headed and run up the stairs with the other more casually dressed agents on his tail.

The elevator doors open, and to my surprise, Agent Clark is already there to greet us. I'm sure that's not part of his duties; he is that sort of guy. And if he ran up the stairs to the third floor, why is he not sweating? And, of course, more realistically, here to join us are the other two agents arriving, slightly panting as regular humans would be expected to do.

I'm following the lead of agent Lora Larson, who has an air of controlled intelligence and knows exactly where to go and when to stop, without even looking at the previous room numbers on the doors as we passed by. Of course, this is not a long hallway. I step aside as Clark and another agent flank the doorway. She knocks and steps aside from the door. Standing right in front of the door is not safe, as you can never tell if a subject might be in a bad mood, may not be open to unexpected visitors, and may be armed. It is better to be safe than sorry.

It's not long before the door opens, and our subject is in a bathrobe, drying his hair with a small white towel. He is surprised to see us all standing in front of him. Agent Larson introduces herself without wasting time as she walks in, fluidly scoping the room with her eyes. Agent Clark walks straight to the balcony area and looks in both directions. He looks back at Agent Larson and simply says

"Clear," in an unmistakable clear voice. The tall agent, still wearing his dark glasses, walks over to the restroom and looks in all directions possible, including the bathtub and shower area, by the sound of the shower curtains moving abruptly. He returns to the room and nods at Agent

Larson, keeping with his silent persona. The other two agents simultaneously walk over into the bedroom area, which is a separate room in this suite, and come back with the "All Clear!"

Now that everybody is aware that nobody else is occupying the room, we can settle down and start asking questions, I'm presuming. He doesn't seem the type of guy who would pose any danger, but do we know for sure? Never assume anything until you have all the evidence. The most innocent-looking individuals have been known to carry out indescribable crimes.

Chapter 19

Interview Or Interrogation

After giving Mr. Jason Lee a moment to put on his clothes, hopefully, the moment of truth was here. I took a chair against the wall, close enough to be in hearing range but not too close to be intrusive in the investigation. After all, I'm no more than an observer and photographer, and I could be considered a consultant.

"Since time is of the essence, I'll get to the matter without hesitation," Lora says as she pulls the chair closer to Mr. Lee.

Is that subliminal intimidation she's using? Mr. Lee is sitting on the corner of the couch, not posing a threat, and his demeanor and expression clearly show that he is as eager as we are to find answers.

Lora asks directly. "Mr. Lee, why were you at the wedding? It has been brought to our attention that you were not an invited guest. What is your connection to the Fontaines, or is it the interest in the bride that brought you there?"

"I know the bride-to-be; at least, I thought I knew her at one point, but things changed suddenly before our wedding took place."

"I see, so you're a jilted lover who may still carry a torch for her and will do anything not to see her get married to another and be happy. Is that what we have here? Where is she, and where did your accomplices take her? We need to know now before she gets hurt, and your attempt at disrupting the service becomes more serious if something happens to her.

"Oh no, you don't understand. I came to warn the family to ensure the wedding didn't occur."

"Well, that much is obvious, but why?" Lora says impatiently.

"She is not who she says she is. We met, and in no time, she became my everything- everything I had ever dreamed of as a partner. She matches my every interest. I couldn't imagine anyone who would be such a perfect mate for me. So, I proposed, and she eagerly accepted. We started making plans for a wedding. I'm the only son, and my parents wanted to give us a wonderful wedding, like the Fontain family wanted to do for their son."

"Okay, great. Will this bring us closer to why you showed up at the Fontaine's? Obviously, your wedding didn't happen, you broke up, maybe she left you at the altar, and you're bitter about it. Now, bring the story to today, why we're here trying to get answers and free a woman from a kidnapping or maybe a worse outcome." Lora's fuse seems shorter by the minute as she unconsciously taps her hand on her sidearm.

Taking a sip of water and following it with a deep breath, Mr. Lee relaxes and consciously focuses on giving Lora a detailed accounting of events. His face transforms from an emotional, nervous subject into an analytical, rational forensic accountant who can relay concise and precise details to get to the bottom of things.

"Special Agent Larson, allow me to explain what I learned, what happened, and how I may help you. I'm a proud man and thought I could handle everything on my own, but I realize I need your assistance as much as you need mine." He says.

"By all means, let's get to it," Lora says, leaning back in her chair.

Mr. Lee continues, "The bottom line is that Jane, who is not her real name, learned all about me and my family by doing extensive research. She infiltrated herself into my life. Lied about her family and the death of her parents in a supposed horrific car accident. She made me feel that I would never meet somebody so perfect for me in my entire life. She manipulated me to no end. Everything was fine; I was in love and looking forward to making her my wife.

My father, a respected and extremely successful business-man, was overjoyed to see me so happy. Nonetheless, he remained a bit suspicious when things were going too well. He insisted on a prenuptial agreement. I argued with him, but when he asked me what I knew about her, my only answer was that I didn't need to know other than I loved her, which was good enough for me. My father spoke with wisdom; he asked me to take some time and ask pertinent questions, like where she was from, what schools she went to, and why I had not met any of her friends. Common things couples share with each other. He made me realize I didn't really know her. I only knew what she wanted me to know. When I started asking questions, her answers deviated, and the more questions I asked, the more defensive she became. I pushed forward and told her my family would love to welcome her into our lives. However, we would sign a prenup before marriage."

Like the rest of us in the room, Lora observes that although Mr. Lee is stoic in recounting the events, he is emotionally charged. She nods and gives him a minute to continue.

After a long sip of water, he clears his throat and pushes forward with renewed resolve.

"My parents were right. As soon as the prenup was brought up, 'Jane' became uncontrollable. She cried, she begged, and she became belligerent and violent. I have never seen somebody change so drastically in my life. It was a revelation of who she truly was and why she showed up in my life when she did." Taking another sip of water and perhaps wishing it were something a little stronger, he forges through.

"A few weeks ago, I was in New Orleans, on business, and that's when I saw an article in The Advocate newspaper, which got my attention. It was a half-page story about Ethan Fontaine's upcoming wedding. On the front page, it showed the unmistakable picture of Jane with Ethan's engagement photo. The story followed on page two. I couldn't believe my eyes; it had been about six months since she disappeared from my life. Through my law enforcement acquaintances, I was able to get some help. Facial recognition technology made it easy to find the trail of death and deceit that trails her.

Chapter 20

Perception Change

"With the bigger picture in view, this information changes everything radically; we're not looking for a victim; we're looking for the perpetrator of many crimes, including murder. Is that what you're saying?

"Yes, I've followed the lead as much as possible. I'm not law enforcement, but without substantiating my research, I knew I would seem like a bitter ex with an ax to grind."

"It's only a matter of time before the Fontaines get a ransom call. After all, only those of us standing in this room know this is not an ordinary kidnapping. Can you brief us on what makes you think this was staged? Or does Jane have a motive?"

"The first case brought to my attention by Facial Rec was one in New Jersey. She had black hair then and married a real estate mogul from Mantoloking. They were married for a little less than three months when he met his untimely death. He was fifteen years her senior but maintained excellent health. He had no history of cardio conditions, yet he died suddenly of an alleged heart attack. The wife requested cremation before performing an autopsy. She inherited his fortune, and since he didn't have children or siblings, no one disputed it. It is obvious she does excellent research on her targets."

"We'll have to substantiate that it is her for sure. We need hard evidence, like fingerprints, to identify and tie her to the events. Anyone else?"

"Yes, I have clippings from Florida, where she married a German national with dual citizenship. Franz Meyer was an exporter of high-end automotive parts. He owned several properties in Munich, Germany, Toledo, Spain, Milan, Italy, and a two-million-dollar penthouse apartment in Miami. He met his death in the ocean, an unfortunate diving accident. The only ones who made it to shore were the red-headed widow and the dive instructor, who nobody could locate after he docked the boat at the exclusive and private Fisher Island harbor."

When is enough, enough? This woman must have more money than she could expend in a hundred lifetimes. The thrill of the hunt and getting away with it must feel like her superpower. I hope that this kidnapping adventure will be her last and that we, and by we, I mean the Special Agents and the law enforcement involved, can put an end to her murderous spree. Put her away for life, where she won't be able to enjoy all her millions.

"We have our work cut out for us. We need to tread lightly. If there is any pressure or mistakes in handling this, Jane can disappear to any of the locations in the world. Never to be found until she commits another crime and, maybe, makes a mistake and gets caught. We cannot leave that to luck or chance. We must be tactful, assertive, and on point with everything we say and do. One oversight and she's off to who knows where. We cannot let that happen. We need all your evidence, notes, and research about this person. We'll take it from here." Lora states, getting up from the chair and giving Jason room to get up.

"Wait a minute, I'm not handing over anything to you. This is personal." Mr. Lee objects.

"That's exactly my point. It is personal, and we cannot have you get in the way or, worse, get hurt on our watch. We appreciate you sharing the information; it's up to us to put the pieces together and get to the bottom of it."

"I need to be a part of this; she did more than break my heart; she took all the trust out of my life; I will never be the same. I need to be a part of stopping her from doing this to anybody else. This is my redemption. I need this."

Lora takes a deep breath and walks to the balcony. Everyone is standing still; there is a charge of electricity throughout the room, and the hair on the back of my neck stands in anticipation. Will Lora consider how he can be an asset to the investigation? After all, he has awareness of intimate details that will aid in the capture of the subject. Or will her ego get in the way and dismiss his devotion and knowledge? This 'Jane' person already discarded him; he doesn't need to be pushed aside yet again.

Exhaling, as she has been holding her breath all this time, Lora calmly says, "Mr. Lee, I'm sure you can provide valuable intel in this situation, but I want you to stay in the background. Do not contact anyone, and do not try to seek information on your own. You will talk to me and only me when you're passing on information that may be relevant. Do not assert yourself, in my case. Or I'll charge you with interfering in a federal investigation and obstruction of justice. Do you understand?"

"But..." he says, a bit more forceful than he might have intended.

"There are no buts...you agree to aid us in a way you're an asset to me, or go back home and stay out of the way. It's all or nothing. Understood? As a matter of fact, it will probably be best if you leave New Orleans. Anything we need from you can be acquired with a phone call. It would be safer for you to go back to Washington and resume work. We appreciate your assistance. We'll be in touch."

Mr. Lee, looking defeated and resigned, opens a briefcase, pulls out three file folders, and hands them to Special Agent Larson.

Larson opens the first folder and skims through the newspaper clippings, photos, and thoroughly typed notes.

You're definitely detail-oriented, which is no surprise. That's why you're such an asset to your team, don't become a liability to mine. Believe me, it is much appreciated. We'll contact you if and when we need you. Have a safe trip."

For the first time, I observe indecision in Lora's eyes. I wonder what that is about. Is she questioning her decision to let Jason leave? I wonder if I'll get close enough to ask her. Or should I mind my own business and stay on as the observer? No, that's not me. I'll ask her as soon as possible. What's the worst that can happen?

Chapter 21

A.S.A.P.

It doesn't look like I will have a chance to ask about her bewildered look. No sooner than we step out of the suite, Lora's phone rings. Underneath her polished exterior, she must have a sense of humor deep inside. Her phone tone is Ding, Ding, from the Law-and-Order series.

"We have to get to the Fontaines' right away. They've received a ransom call. The cards are in our favor. The challenging thing is to convince the Fontaines, especially Ethan, that this whole thing is a ruse to extort money from them," she says, hurrying to the elevator. "Get ready for the storm."

"After you share with them what happened to the others who were not so fortunate as to have a prenup, I'm sure they'll be content with playing along and have the opportunity to stop this girl from repeating her unscrupulous acts."

"No, I meant a real storm. Look at those cumulus dark clouds. We can't take a chance driving the causeway. It may be closed by the time we get there. We'll arrange for a helicopter to take us there; it will cut the time in half."

Without missing a beat, she calls out to Agent Clark, who walks past us, a bit ahead of the crowd, and standing ready.

"Clark, get the State Police to meet us at Lakefront airport. We'll need to hitch a ride on their Helo. See if Senior Trooper Elias Collins is available. Good ol' "Slick" owes me one."

"Would you care to elaborate? 'Slick'? I question.

"That's a conversation we can have over a glass of wine once we take care of business."

"Fair enough, I look forward to it," I say with renewed curiosity.

"It looks like you're coming with us on the helicopter ride. Don't get airsick, do you? I'm sure the Fontaines will feel more at ease with your familiar face among the chaos."

"Actually, I love to fly. I have a fixed-wing license—it may be a little dusty, but you know what they say: It's like riding a bicycle, just a little more air between the pedals and the ground," I say proudly.

Lora acknowledges my comment with a slight smile and then continues the discussion without interruption. "The challenging part is to have them play along with the kid-nappers to lure them in the right direction towards apprehension. It is challenging to have civilians manipulating criminals to cooperate with them rather than the other way around. After all, any sign that we know what they're up to, and they could disappear and go somewhere to find another unsuspecting victim.

Lora's phone dings. She answers before the second ding. "Larson, yes, connect me. Hi, 'Slick', can you fly us? "Clicking the button on the speaker, she looks and winks at me. I wonder what that's all about, and in an instant, I know why. 'Slick has a delightful Cajun-tinged jargon, and I can't help but smile even in the face of the serious dilemma at hand.

"Can you meet us at Lakefront tarmac?"

"I sure can, now don't you keep me waitin'," He says, chuckling.

"What do you mean? We're around the corner from the airport.

"I happened to drop somebody off at the terminal; when I got the call, I re-fueled, got a cup of coffee, inspected the bird, and am now chit-chatting. By the way, get here as quickly as possible, our window for a safe take-off is closing in. Never you mind, I hear your sirens."

It's incredible how having lights and sirens, going Code 3, cuts travel time in less than half. Usually, getting from the Laffitte Hotel would take about fifteen minutes or more, depending on the traffic. After all, it is approximately eight miles away. However, we are in a hurry to get there and do our due diligence in our mission.

It's too bad we drove by the most beautiful terminal I've seen at such speed. We went by so fast that the Art Deco Angels encased in the façade of the building seemed to be flying. I'll have to come back and visit on a more leisurely adventure.

We drive onto the airfield through the back gates. Apparently, they are expecting us, and they know we're in a hurry. The SUB pulls up short of the helicopter. Lora opens the door and jumps out. I'm sure Clark has not shifted gears into park yet. I exit with a bit more caution and move to the back of the vehicle, where Lora is going through a black tactical bag. Will she hand me a weapon in case things get rough?

"Here, take this, we're going to need it."

There is no firearm for me. It's a rain poncho folded neatly in an envelope-style black bag. Upon taking it out, I see the FBI stamped across the back in white letters. Now, I feel special and official. While inspecting my rain gear, I see she's throwing her high-heeled shoes in the back and putting on a pair of boots. Oh my, I don't think the storm is going to be that bad. So far, there haven't been any raindrops.

"Good to see you again, Slick. It's been too long—this is Jessica Martin. She's been an unexpected asset in this case." Lora says, with an elegant wave of her hand in my direction.

"Senior Trooper Collins, Pilot-Command, at your service, ma'am." He says with a slight bow.

"Nice to meet you, Commander Collins, but if you call me ma'am, I'm just going to have to call you 'Slick' even though I haven't heard the story behind the nickname.

"Fair enough, I won't call you ma'am, but you can still call me 'Slick' if you like; after all, we may become really close friends with this adventure we're embarking on." Now, you don't mind—get in the Chopper before the tower shuts us down for take-off."

The storm clouds are way in the distance, and it's not even raining yet. The wind is more like a soft, warm breeze. I don't feel this impending doom. However, who am I to argue with trained flying professionals? As I mentioned before, my pilot's license may be dusty. Oh well, let me get in my seat and buckle up in case it becomes a bumpy ride.

The co-pilot has already started the cycling process to warm up the rudders, and we're ready to take off. As 'Slick' looks back and gives the four of us in the back the thumbs up, the rain comes down, as if somebody is throwing a bucket of water on the Helo. Where did the rain come from? And am I glad Lora gave me the poncho? After all, a firearm would not keep me dry in this deluge.

Chapter 22

Storm?

Inside the cockpit of Bayou Six-One, the rain taps against the windshield like impatient woodpeckers searching for grub. Lightning strikes the lake beyond the airfield. Instruments glow faintly—artificial horizon, altimeter, radar—all lit like the cockpit with surreal, ghostly glow. In a matter of seconds, the storm has engulfed us, and there is no turning back. We're on a mission.

Slick adjusted his headset, voice cool and clipped. "Lakefront Tower, Helicopter Bayou Six-One, IFR to Mandeville. Ready to copy clearance."

The response crackled through the static-filled comms. "Bayou Six-One, you are cleared to Mandeville Regional via direct, maintain 1,500 feet. Expect 3,000 five minutes after departure. Departure frequency 124.2. Squawk 4327."

Slick repeated it without missing a beat. "Cleared to Mandeville direct, maintain 1,500, expect 3,000 after five, 124.2, squawk 4327. Bayou Six-One."

Lora adjusts her headset and asks. "We good? As she fixes her eyes on the thickening clouds ahead.

"Nothing to worry about, I've flown in worse." He says that maintaining a calm, professional, and controlled voice, pilots practice for hours, to keep calm among the passengers in the worst of scenarios.

The helicopter lifts light and smooth, and its rotor wash stirs the standing rain. We pierce the soup of gray sky, and the impenetrable cloud cover instantly swallows us.

"Bayou Six-One, radar contact. Proceed direct, maintain heading one-one-zero. Contact New Orleans Approach."

"Copy that, Tower. Bayou Six-One switching to Approach."

This precarious situation is bringing back memories of my flying days back in California. Although the weather was seldom an issue, the amount of traffic that filled the airways was. The other problem was the proximity to the airspace of the various super-busy airports. Once you get to the desired altitude, there is no feeling like it. The freedom of flying. The stillness and feeling of gliding like a bird. And the unexpected moments of panic that would spring out of nowhere when another plane would cross your trajectory simply because they were on VFR, Visual

Flight Rules, and had not filed a flight plan. All you would hear on the radio is "Target a 12 o'clock altitude unknown, keep an eye out. Acknowledge when you have a visual. Like I said, moments of absolute panic until you see the target and can avert it. Then all is calm once more, well, at least once your heart has slowed down enough to take a breath.

The memories fade instantly as a gust of wind hits us. I'm hoping it is just a wind gust and not wind shear. I trust Slick to pull us through, and hope that we'll live another day so he can tell me the story of how he got his nickname over a nice cold Abita beer.

The wind off Lake Pontchartrain carries the sharp smack of rain, thickening by the minute.

The helicopter lurches like a piñata under siege by a mob of sugar-starved ten-year-olds.

Lightning flares—brief and blinding—turning the sky to daylight, then dunking it in ink.

Thunder crashes hard enough to make the rivets rattle, the whole frame shuddering as if ready to come undone. But the worst sound is the fuselage creaking—moaning under pressure—as the bird gets tossed side to side like prey in an alligator's jaws, seconds before the death roll.

The storm is getting worse by the minute. How long until we land? I hate to be that person, but I have to ask. "Slick, are we there yet?" I ask meekly into my headset.

Bayou Six-One slices through sheets of rain. I'm peeking in between the two agents sitting across from us into the cockpit, which glows like a war room--red lights, fast blinks, urgent beeps.

"Bayou Six-One, IFR cancellation received. Radar services terminated. Maintain VFR. Good luck down there." The ghostly and assuring voice comes through the comm for one last transmission.

"Copy, ATC. Cancelling IFR. Bayou Six-One out." Assured and confident sounding, our Commander answers.

Slick holds the cyclic stick, eyes narrowing. "Alright, people. We're on our own—we're going eyeballs and instincts from here."

From the back, Agent Clark leans forward, knuckles white as he taps Lora's knee and gives her a reassuring smile.

"You see the house yet?" Lora asks.

"I see something," Slick muttered. "Let's hope it's not a gazebo."

Lightning slashed across the sky, illuminating the drenched sprawl of the Fontaine estate. The once-manicured lawn is now a churned mess of mud and standing water, fenced by live oaks swaying like they want to slap the helo from the sky.

I clutched the seatbelt and got the rain poncho at the ready to throw over my head. I'm glancing at Agent Larson—she is stone-faced and unreadable—as if storm landings are just Tuesday morning yoga.

The silent agent remained just that: silent. I'm beginning to think he may be an experimental bot. If he starts rusting, we'll know for sure.

"We're coming in hot," Slick announced. "Someone better warn their landscaping team."

The helicopter dips, rotors whining against the wind. Rain claws at the windshield. The ground rises much too fast, and the clearing is too narrow. The tail sways—Slick corrects.

"One shot," he muttered. "No go-arounds."

With a final blast of turbine, the skids drop onto the lawn with bone-rattling thud and a skid—mud splatters everywhere, rotor wash flattening trees.

"We're down!"

Lora pops the buckle. "Let's go!"

We all bail out into the downpour, sprinting low under the spinning rotors. Rain plasters hair to faces, soaks every inch. I'm running and throwing the poncho over my head. The wind catches the edge, and it shoves it up against my face, leaving me disoriented and uncovered from the waist down and soaking my jeans. Shoes sink into wet grass that has all the consistency of soup.

The back door of the Fontaine house burst open.

The storm is behind us, or is it?

Chapter 23

From One Storm To Another

We enter the house. The staff hears the chopper and springs into action. They wield large, fluffy white towels, which will quickly lose their pristine color. We take a minute to compose ourselves after our harrowing flight in. Water pools around us as we stand, making the marble floors slippery and hazardous. But have no fear—here comes Anne, the house manager, and two young girls with mops and more towels that they spread on the floors.

It is humorous how these same agents would rush into a building, guns blazing, to rescue, apprehend, and save a life or two. Yet, we stand here paralyzed as we cannot imagine traipsing through such a grand home and messing it up with our water-soaked clothes, mud, and debris.

Somehow, Lora's poncho did the job and kept her from getting drenched. She only had to remove her boots, which she set aside, and put on a pair of flat shoes she pulled out of her oversized black bag. I wonder if she has a spear pair. Clark removes his Chelsey boots, which apparently kept his feet dry, and moves out of the area. And, of course, Agent Silent, for some reason, doesn't appear to be wet at all. There is something off-putting about him, and before this is over, I will find out what it is.

Well, folks, I feel awful, but my jeans are completely soaked, and since I threw on a light wool jacket this morning to appear professional, I now smell like a sheep. Just when I thought the day could not get any worse.

So far, the agents have proceeded to the drawing room, where the family has congregated, and will share the new revelations.

Meanwhile, I stand here shivering and wondering what to do next. Fortunately, Anne reads my discomfort and ushers me from the kitchen to one of the guest rooms.

As I leave the kitchen, the back door opens with a bang against the wall, and Slick and the co-pilot make an apologetic entrance.

"I'm so sorry about that. That wind just took the door from me, and I apologize."

"Not a problem." Chef Henrie says, moving towards the men and handing them towels.

"I hate to impose, but we are grounded until the storm passes. We'll be out of your hair as soon as it does."

Chef Henrie escorts the men into the kitchen's eating area. "Please sit and make yourselves comfortable. I'll get you something to eat. I'm sure that flight gave you an appetite."

As I look back, it looks like the Commander and his co-pilot are taken care of, so now it's my turn to get out of these wet clothes and join the others. I do not want to miss anything.

"Jessica, let me get you a robe, and I'll wash and dry your clothes as soon as possible. That way, you can join the others in a bit. I'm sure the Fontaines will be pleased to see you."

"I feel terrible; the poncho was dysfunctional; it was supposed to keep me dry, like the one agent Larson wore, but mine just flipped up and displayed me to the elements as if it was possessed." I must be present, especially when they tell Ethan the truth about Jane. I can't sit here and wait for my clothes to dry."

I tie the fluffy white luxury robe around tightly to prevent further embarrassment, and I put on the matching fluffy slippers Anne provided for me.

"I'm going to join them; I can't miss this. Please let me know when the clothes are dry. Thank you so much."

Before I leave the room, Anne calls me and hands me a small glass of Sherry. "This will put you at ease as you stroll in with your luxury comfort wear, like a golden era movie star."

"I feel more like an alcoholic polar bear, but I'll go with your vision," I say, smiling and getting my resolve.

Chapter 24

A Robe And Fluffy Slippers

I don't think of myself as a head-turner, but judging by the glances, I'm making one now—in a robe and fluffy slippers, no less. I could cower and slink out of the room, or I can own it. Smile. Walk in. Sit down. Be present. I choose the latter. I don't run from discomfort—especially not today.

"Please continue," I say, steady and clear. "I'm here if you need me."

Agent Lora Larson nods. "I'm glad you're here. We were going over things with the detectives."

Mrs. Fontaine chimes in, her voice delicate, careful. "There was a phone call. A man, disguised voice. Said they had Jane."

"When I asked to speak to her," Ethan adds, his voice cracking, "they said they'd call back. That was over an hour ago."

The air shifts. A silent snap of tension that tightens everyone's posture. This is it. The moment that separates the before from the after.

Lora steps forward, centered and composed, but I can see the slight set of her jaw. She's done this before. The kind of delivery that turns someone's life upside down.

"Ethan," she says gently, "can you take a seat?"

He doesn't move. Just locks eyes with Agent Larson, like he's bracing for a punch.

I shift in my seat. Damp strands of hair cling to the back of my neck, and for the first time since I stepped into this house, I forget I'm wrapped in a luxury robe. Lora's measured, sorrowful words hush the room, making the silence press in.

"We've confirmed the identity and motive of the woman you were about to marry."

Ethan's shoulders stiffen.

"No," he snaps. "What I want to know is why you're still here instead of out looking for Jane. You've already wasted a day! There's a storm—so what? I need her back!"

He's not angry, he's unraveling.

"Ethan..." Lora's tone sharpens just enough to cut through his panic. "Jane isn't who she said she was. She lied—to you, to your family. Everything about her was a lie."

He bolts upright. "That's not true!"

Agent Silent moves, smooth and quiet as fog, intercepting without touching. Just presence. Lora lifts a hand—let him breathe.

I catch a glimpse of the look in her eyes—regret laced with professional distance.

"She's done this before," Lora says. "At least three times. The third man—the one who came to your wedding to warn you—he wasn't lying. He was one of her victims."

That man. I flash back to his face—desperate, bruised, trying to convey to Ethan what he was getting into. I could see in the video's close-up. The look in his eyes wasn't madness; it was grief.

"The other two." Lora continues. "Dead. Within months of marrying her."

Ethan falters backward, his knees give, and he collapses onto the couch. His hands clutch his face, but not fast enough to hide the devastation breaking through.

Mrs. Fontaine is there in seconds, wrapping him in her arms, but there are things even a mother can't make right.

My heart aches. I've photographed a hundred weddings, seen a thousand 'forevers' start with hope and smiles. This situation is what it looks like when one ends in betrayal.

Mrs. Fontaine's voice trembles. "Are you certain? Couldn't someone be trying to sabotage her? She seemed so lost. Like she needed us. I thought"

Lora's voice softens. "I'm sorry. I know it's hard to believe. But this wasn't about love. It was about money. Access. Control. When the prenup came into play, it changed everything."

"The man who showed up at the wedding and tried to convey the truth," Lora continues. "He got suspicious. His parents pushed for a prenup, and after they signed it, she vanished. Moved on. Fast."

Lora leans forward slightly, her tone firm but not unkind. "Ethan... believe it or not, you were the one who got away."

And there it is—the truth, out in the open, sharp and unrelenting.

Ethan doesn't speak. He stares at nothing, hollow-eyed, lost somewhere between fury and heartbreak.

I sit in silence, resisting the urge to go to him. I barely know Ethan, but I know what betrayal looks like. I've captured it on film—moments too raw for the lens. But this one, this is personal. And it's far from over.

Chapter 25

Clear For Take-Off

Anne taps me on the shoulder and whispers. "Your clothes are dry, Miss Jessica."

"Thank you so much," I reply, conflicted. Part of me is glad my clothes are dry, and the other is sad because I have to abandon this fabulous, warm, luxurious robe and fluffy slippers. I wish this were a hotel, and I could take them home as part of their hospitality giveaways.

Everybody moves simultaneously to carry on in whatever capacity they need to be and do. The Fontaines move into the sitting room, a much cozier and warmer place. I'm sure they need time alone to digest both the horror and, at the same time, the relief the truth brought to them. Once the realization sets in, they may even be grateful. Even though Ethan is heartbroken, which is a temporary situation, at least he is alive. If he had married the She-Devil, chances are he would have become yet another statistic of a husband who died under uncertain circumstances. The Fontaines' nightmare would be a permanent one.

It's a good feeling to get back into my clothes. I don't know what Anne did to the jacket, but it does not smell like it came from a sheep croft in Scotland.

Slick is waving at me from the kitchen entrance, motioning me to go to him. I wonder what he has to share.

"What's up, Slick?"

"We are... the storm has passed, and even though another one is on its way, we are clear for take-off within a forty-minute window."

"What's with these storms? I don't remember them being so close together or this severe."

"One thing that is always constant is change. You can bank on that." He smirks.

"I'll be ready to go in five. I must say bye to the Fontaines and ensure they're okay. I do need to get back home to my little ones."

"I didn't know you had kids..."

"A dog and a cat, TK and TC—they get an attitude if I stay away too long."

"I get it; I get the same from the Mrs," he chuckles.

✳

I knock gently on the arch leading to the room where the family has gathered. I don't know the name of this room or its function, but it has a beautiful, inviting fireplace and large arched windows overlooking the lagoon. On the opposite side is a wall of bookshelves. I know it's not the library, as that room is much larger and has two fireplaces. The Fontaines enjoy reading, as there are books in almost every room of this grand residence.

"Please come in, Jessica. Can I get you something?" says Mrs. Fontaine, the ultimate hostess, getting up from the couch and coming over to me.

"I just came to see how you are before I head out. The commander said more weather is coming, but we have a safe window to get home before the second storm arrives."

"We are dealing with the circumstances; this is unbearable for Ethan. And as a mother, it's breaking my own heart. How can somebody be so heartless?" she whispers.

"I can't answer that. If I understood Jane's motive, I'd be a monster like her." I whisper back. I don't want Ethan to hear me calling her a monster. After all, Ethan was profoundly in love with this woman. "May I say bye to Ethan?"

"Of course," she says, putting her hand in mine and walking towards the fireplace, where Ethan is sitting in a high-backed chair staring into the crackling flames.

"Ethan, I'm so sorry you're going through this. I know you're hurting. One thing I know is that you're loved by many. Your family is here for you. That is priceless. I hope you consider me a friend and know I'm also here for you. I will do whatever I can to help. You got my word."

Ethan looks up at me and rises from the chair. There is a millisecond of uncertainty in his eyes before he extends his arms and hugs me. He holds me as he breaks down and sobs on my shoulder.

Was this the storm the commander was talking about?

I let him cry and release the pain. There are no words that I could say to make it better. All I can do is tap gently on his back, comforting him as a child awoken from a nightmare.

I step back slightly, releasing the hold. Ethan also steps back and says something unexpected.

"I'm glad you said we're friends, or I would feel backward hugging a stranger like that," he says with a shy smile, averting his eyes back to the fire.

He has embarked on the healing path, which starts with humor, at least in my world. As I walk away, I can only say, "I'm here for you, all of you. "

I'm going to the library, which the law-enforcement hub has turned into its command center. I must let Special Agent Larson know I'll be heading back to town. I'm sure this goodbye won't be quite as emotional—unless Agent Silent decides to hug me—somehow, I don't think that will be happening.

Chapter 26

Keeping The Poncho

As we head to the helicopter, I take in the aftermath of the storm. To my surprise, the trees that once looked ready to snap are standing tall again, their branches stretching toward the sun as if welcoming a second chance. The ground drinks up the puddles like a thirsty sponge. Overhead, the sky is a vivid cerulean--blissfully unaware that the storm might circle back for round two.

I catch sight of the co-pilot, busy with his pre-flight inspection. I realize I never caught his name—too much rush, too much adrenaline when we first boarded. He moves with precision, clearly someone who takes his role seriously. The least I can do is show the same respect.

"Slick," I say, matching his pace toward the chopper, "I've been meaning to ask—what's the co-pilot's name?

In all the, let's call it excitement of earlier, we skipped the formal intros."

"You're right," Slick replies. "We just piled in and got out of Dodge. His name's Skyler. Skyler Thomson. And before you ask—no nickname. A pilot named Skyler doesn't need one."

I smile at that, then angle toward the co-pilot as he closes an inspection panel and turns, catching our approach.

"Skyler Thomson?" I ask, offering a hand. "I'm Jessica Martin. I meant to introduce myself earlier, but we were a little short on pleasantries."

He takes my hand with a firm but easy grip, nodding. "Good to meet you, Jessica."

"I appreciate the thorough pre-flight. Looks like you don't leave much to chance."

"No chance of that," he says with a half-smile, eyes flicking back to the bird.

"Glad to be in good hands," I say, hopping aboard, looking forward to flying back under clear skies.

As I disembark Bayou Six-One, I feel a pang of nostalgia. Is it the fact that we survived a treacherous adventure together that somehow bonded us for life? Maybe it's just me. I am sure these two flying mavericks and law enforcement elites, who have flown on many perilous missions, won't even give it a second emotional thought. I gather my purse and my not-so-handy poncho and step down to the tarmac. I know, the poncho felt short, but it has FBI emblazoned on it, I'm keeping it.

"Jessica, where is your ride?" Thompson asks as he gathers his flight bag.

"It is parked at the FBI building parking lot. I rode with Special Agent Larson into the Quarter, and from there we came here. I'm sure I can get a taxi or Uber. After all, it can't be more than a mile and a half from here." I say, not wanting to impose.

"Slick let's give Jessica a ride back to her car, it's on the way to the station," Thompson says, as if saying no is not an option.

"Sure thing, we're off and heading back to the station—got a few reports to write and then home sweet home for 24 hours. Unless there is an emergency call. Our headquarters is in Baton Rouge, as you may know, but we do have an office we work out of, by the Ceasars Superdome. It's on our way, and that way you can get home to the kids..." Slick says, smirking as though we're sharing a private joke.

Without missing a beat. Thompson asks, "You have kids?"

"As a matter of fact, I do, TK and TC," I say, going along with what Slick already started.

"TK and TC? Kind of peculiar names for kids," he says, raising an eyebrow at Slick.

Holding back laughter, I say, "TK stands for Tiny K-9, and TC is Tiny Cat. They're my kids," I say, grinning at Slick.

Sitting in the back of the State Police SUV--thankfully without cuffs--I realize it was only yesterday that I was looking forward to photographing a gorgeous wedding, surrounded by happy people.

Today was a whirlwind--leaving the house with intel for the FBI, getting the truth from Jason, flying through a violent storm, and unleashing a tempest of pain and betrayal. It all feels like a nightmare. For my part, I've hit pause, pulled myself from chaos, and I'm ready to get my life back on track. Tomorrow is Monday, and I recall a meeting on the calendar with a new client, the owner of one of the Haunted Mansions just outside of town. Tourists love that stuff, and whether people believe in ghosts or not, they love the adrenaline that goes with a good haunt. I know I will capture the perfect atmospheric shots to draw them in.

"Here we are, your chariot awaits," Slick announces, getting me out of my head for a second, and letting me out of the back seat, since the doors don't open from the inside.

"Well, thank you, gentlemen, for the flight and the ride. I so appreciate it. Stay safe!"

"Before you go--here is my card, I've written my cell on the back," Slick says

If you ever need to fly somewhere, keep me or Thompson in mind. I have a feeling you're not your typical civilian. You are a former forensic photographer back in LA. That makes you one of us. And you know what they say...Once a cop..."

"I'm going to stop you now, I've made it so far, without getting misty, and I won't start now. I appreciate it, and you're right—according to my friend Robert, with the FBI, I do have a knack for trouble. If I need you, I'll call." I say and give him a slight side hug.

Halfway to my car, I turn and yell before he gets back in his vehicle. "Hey, don't forget, you still haven't told me why they call you 'Slick."

"That's right," he replies. "You've got the number. Call me--we'll get some beers, and I'll tell you the story."

Chapter 27

Client Meeting Re-scheduled

Waking up in my comfortable bed, snuggling with my purring TC, and snoring TK contrasts with yesterday's events.

I'm glad I scheduled the appointment with my new client, Evette Larue, for 11:30; that gives me plenty of time to enjoy my morning.

I stretch, laughing as the furballs leap across the bed and onto each other—and then, of course, onto me.

Okay, it's time to get up and saunter to the kitchen, where the unmistakable aroma of my favorite Chicory Coffee beckons me fully awake.

"Oh no, the phone—so early." I glance at the unknown number and answer, still in my morning haze.

"Good morning!"

"Jessica?"

"Yes, this is she."

"Hi! Sorry if I woke you—this is Evette Larue."

"Oh—no worries, I'm up."

"Great. Any chance we can meet earlier? Like 9:30? My schedule's slammed, and I may not have another opening for a week or two."

Okay, so this morning will not be leisurely for me or my pet crew. I must switch gears, get it together, and be at the coffee shop in about an hour.

"Sure, that's not a problem. I can meet you at Mon Cherie Coffee Shop at 9:30. I look forward to it. See you then," I say, sipping coffee between breaths and pouring kibble into the bowls for the tiny, hungry beasties. Let's not forget to fill up their water bowls.

Hoping in the shower, I wonder why the turn of events went from leisurely to frantic in no time. I let the water cleanse my anxiety and clear my head.

This opportunity could be financially rewarding because she advertises a lot, and her ads are clearly dated. We both win if I can match her urgency with my creative photographic talent. And I need this win. Since the death of DuBois, business has dwindled. I hadn't realized how much work he funneled my way through the various venues owned by NOLA's Tourist Tours and all their marketing campaigns. That reminds me, I must touch base with Thomas, the assistant, actually, the new owner of NOLA's Tourist Tours. I miss that guy. However,

I must now concentrate on the new client, Ms. Evette Larue—time to move forward and do it at lightning speed.

Made it. The Fleur-de-Lis clock clicks to 9:30 as I slip into the café. I'm looking around to get the best seat facing the entrance, so I don't miss her coming in. The aroma of freshly baked goodies attacks my taste buds instantly. That's why this is my favorite place for first meetings. Even if the meeting goes south, it is a sweet experience. This is the first time I'll meet the client, and I hope I recognize her. I only know her from her advertisement photos—a pleasant-looking middle-aged blonde. As I scan the place, I can't help but notice a lady with a jet-black bob haircut waving me over. I immediately realize it's my client. Is she revamping her look? Or is she running from the law? I'll try not to act surprised and see if she volunteers an explanation.

"Good morning, Ms. La Rue, how you feeling?" I say with my typical New Orleans greeting.

"In a hurry as always, trying to fit too many things in one day. You know how that is when you run your own business. It never stops."

No sooner than I sit down, the waitress, Beatrice, comes running over and places two cafés au lait in front of us and two croissants. Probably what I was going to order. I didn't expect somebody I've never met to order for me. That's intrusive. Not sure how I feel about it. No wasting time looking at the menu or deciding what to get. This lady may have some control issues. Let's smile and thank her for being so intuitive instead. I don't want to ruffle her feathers and lose the gig before it takes flight.

"Well, thank you. You must have read my mind. Let's get down to business and share with me what you're looking for in your marketing campaign." I pull out my tablet to jot down some notes.

This lady has come prepared as she reaches into her shiny black alligator leather tote, big enough to carry a live alligator in it. She pulls out a massive file containing magazine pages, photographs, drawings, and numerous pages with lists.

"Oh, you may have noticed my look has changed from the previous marketing brochures. I played a minor part as the face of the company, and my previous partner was more of the aesthetic focus. She was a model in her younger years and thought it was only natural for her to continue taking center stage. Since she is no longer with the company, I did most of the work myself. I thought, Why not? I changed my look to fit in with the Gothic atmosphere of the Mansions and bring to life something magical and mysterious. Don't you think?"

To me, she has her mind made up about how things need to look and be. There is not much room for discussion. Sometimes, it is better to listen than to speak, and this is one of those occasions. So, I smile, nod, and take notes. I can't help wondering what happened to her old partner, and should I be looking for a fresh-dug grave when taking pictures of the garden?

"I'd like you to come down to Mansion La Rue and take about 30 photos in the various rooms and outside of the house. After that, if I'm satisfied with how you capture the ambiance of what I'm looking for, we can discuss a fee. Nes pas?"

She really wants to run the show, and do I want to be one of her players? I need the business, but my gut asks, Is it worth it?

"Before we take that step, I would like to share with you some of the shots I've taken of some mansions around the city. Before we spend travel time, you can see my style and see if it's a fit. After all, I may already have what you're looking for. Of course, I am familiar with your mansions, and they are unique and gorgeous, and they have a certain air of mystery that draws you in."

I look to make eye contact and convey this is not a one-sided arrangement; I see her staring at the door as if in a trance. Of course, I turn to see what she is fixating on. A woman who could be her identical twin enters the shop. The lady stares at her for a beat and then directs her vision to me, glaring as she hurriedly returns outside and runs away. It is in that instant that I recognize her. A jolt spikes through me, Jane Douth, in the flesh. I got to go. Left behind is my untouched mouth-watering warm croissant and undrunk coffee. I grab my tablet and shout back, "I'll call you."

Chapter 28

Is It Her?

Where the heck did, she go? I'm looking to the right, and I'm looking to the left, but I cannot spot her anywhere. Even across the street, there is no sign of her. How did she vanish so quickly? I know I wasn't imagining things. She obviously recognized me and had a fight-or-flight response; why else would she take off in such a hurry? Ok, let's look at this logically. Easier said than done when the adrenaline is pumping. She didn't have time to run across the street. I was on her tail in seconds. She did not get into a car and drive away; no cars had moved from this block since I came outside. She must have docked at one of the stores on this block. If I keep scanning back and forth like this, I'll sprain my neck. Time to cross the street. From this point of view, I can watch the entire short block at once. Well, a few high-profile vehicles are obstructing my view, but I'll give it a try and see if I can spot her coming out.

Fantastic. I left La Rue mid-rant. If she sees me skulking on the other side of the street, she'll assume I ghosted her. Which, honestly, was tempting. But I'd rather not lose a paying client with deep pockets and a short fuse. The way the one-sided conversation was going gave me more than one reason for leaving, but I really didn't want to jeopardize my chances with her. She may be challenging, but I can work with her. I've had worse clients. I can't remember when, but I'm sure I've had them. I'll have to think of some super excuse for leaving, like the house was on fire, and I hope she is open to an apology.

I must find the so-called Jane Douth. She must have ducked into one of the shops. She couldn't have gotten far—unless there's a back exit I don't know about. How is this block set up? A couple of the stores have courtyards and apartments in the back. She could have left out the back door and gone across to the other side of the block, in which case she's in the wind—so close and yet so far away.

Oh wow, she is coming out of the clothing boutique a few doors from the coffee shop. She thinks I can't spot her because she put on big dark glasses and a silk scarf around her head. Where is the convertible? I must tell her the 60s called; they want the scarf back.

I'm crossing the street, yet again, and covertly following without letting her see me. She turned and looked up and down the block to check if someone was following her. She's either paranoid or knows she's up to no good. Glad I was on the other side of the street, behind the Hummer. Now, I want to watch her without following too closely. I need to know where she's going, where she is staying, and if she is alone. She can't pull off these high-end coercive ops on her own. After all, she received assistance during the wedding to exit and create the appearance of being taken away. I'm sure she didn't hire movers by the hour. Nobody sticks their neck out in the commission of a crime without having a stake in it. There has to be a payout worth risking going to prison.

I wonder if she has an actual destination in mind or if she's going to wander until she hits the edge of the Quarter. Maybe I've lost my touch. Does she know I'm following her?

That's ridiculous.

Ok—time to strategize. If Jane ducks into a restaurant, do I follow? Watch from the street? I need a plan. I must prepare for the unexpected, especially with someone like her.

There's another boutique coming up. I'm dying to see if Jane slips in and reemerges in a new scarf. Gotta stay sharp. She's a chameleon.

The sun's relentless, the humidity's crawling down my neck, and I never even got to eat that darn croissant. It's starting to get to me.

Wait—no way. She just walked into NOLA's Tourist Tours.

I couldn't ask for more.

Thomas doesn't even know he's about to become my eyes and ears. Maybe she's booking a boat, or taking an unsuspecting mark into the Bayou on an airboat joyride to a dead-end.

Time to cross the street, one more time, find some shade, and disappear into the background while I keep watch.

Chapter 29

To Follow Or Not

D o I follow her, or find out what she's already left behind for me?

There she is—emerging from NOLA's Tourist Tours, slipping her sunglasses back on. I can't blame her; with the sun blaring overhead, it's less a fashion statement or disguise and more a survival tool. This shop keeps its interiors dim, casting a mysterious, welcoming vibe, but out here, the midday glare demands protection.

Jane doesn't get far. No sooner does she step onto the curb than a vehicle pulls up and scoops

her away. She must have called ahead; the timing is too perfect to be a coincidence, and I'm not a fan of coincidences, but rather probabilities to discover.

Phone ready, I crouch low behind a parked car and snap a shot of the getaway vehicle—or try to.

My heart sinks — no license plate.

Once again, she vanishes in plain sight.

Funny how things come full circle. I've been thinking about reaching out to Thomas, and now here I am — pushed by circumstance.

I'll talk to Mr. Thomas Dupris and apologize for being a ghost for way too long. After we hug it out—we'll do lunch.

Visions of my abandoned croissant still dance through my head.

It's been a while since Thomas risked his life to help me. I'm not about to come charging in, demanding answers about what Jane may or may not have said.

I need to fill him in and let him decide if he wants to share anything — if there's anything to share.

Eyes adjusting to the gloom, I move carefully through the shop, avoiding a full-body collision with a precarious display.

Mental note: suggest a few more sconces. Either that or bring night-vision goggles next time.

"Thomas, you in here?" I call, scanning the dusky interior—no sign of him.

My heartbeat kicks up a notch as I make my way toward the back. Dark thoughts creep in — flashes of blood, lifeless bodies, crime scenes burned into my mind from my old life—some things you never unsee.

The phone rings — sharp, insistent. No answer.

That's not good.

I quicken my pace, pushing through the curtain over the archway — and smack straight into Thomas, earbuds blaring so loud I can hear the thump of the bass battling my own pulse.

"Jessica! What a surprise!" he says, tugging out his earbuds, blissfully unaware he just shaved a year off my life. "What's wrong? You look pale, like you've seen a ghost."

"I'm just glad I didn't," I say, exhaling. "I saw someone leave the shop, and when I couldn't find you, my mind... went places."

"Oh, honey, I'm fine. Better than ever!" Thomas beams. "Why would you think that sweet thing who just left would hurt me? She's a dear. Just met her, and I think we'll be besties.

Not to mention" he leans in, "—she rented a 100-foot luxury yacht for a week at 150 K plus through the Yachts R Us franchise. Not their real name, but I call them that. It's like a toy store for everything nautical. Big boats. Big fun." Grinning away, he continues. "The deposit or APA, which stands for Advance Provisioning Allowance, is 20%. Just in case you're not familiar with seafaring terminology. I get ten percent commission on the entire package. So, Miss Janet Jones has become my best friend."

"Janet Jones, you say?—interesting," I say, taking a breath before I blow his bubble.

His exuberance is contagious, but there's a cold knot in my stomach. I need to set the record straight about his new "bestie gently."

"Thomas, think you can get out of here for a bit?"

"One of the perks of being my own boss," he grins. "I'd love to catch up."

"Great. I'm buying. And no time limits — we've got a lot of ground to cover. Starting with my apology for falling off the face of the earth."

"Oh, darlin', don't even think about it," he says, flipping the 'Be Back' sign with a flourish. "After all that went down with Antoine's death, and you framed by that snake of a detective... It was like quicksand. Once we climbed out, we all needed to breathe. Let's leave it in the past."

"Where to?" I ask as we step outside.

"How about Mr. Ed's on Royal Street? Great food, friendly faces."

"Sounds perfect. And just checking—the restaurant doesn't have any talking horses in the back, do they?"

I grin, hoping he'll catch the ancient pop-culture reference.

Thomas chuckles, and for the first time in a long time, things almost feel normal.

Normal's a pretty word. Too bad in my world, it never sticks around for long.

Chapter 30

Let's Do Lunch

"Are you sure we're talking about the same person? Before you go on, I must sit down and have a drink." Thomas huffs, not from our three-block stroll—but from sheer anxiety.

"I can assure you; it's her. I spotted her at Mon Cherrie Coffee Shop while I was meeting a client. She walked in, and we locked eyes for a split second--long enough for us to recognize each other. She bolted like her fake hair was on fire. She's a trickster, a gold digger, and a murderer—and honestly, those might be her better qualities."

"But she seems so nice and open," Thomas says, shaking his head in disbelief.

"This person, whatever her name is, is dangerous. I don't know what she's planning next. She knows I saw her, but she doesn't know I stayed on her tail all the way to your shop. It looks like she's gearing up for another scam. As far as I know, she's still working the kidnapping angle with the Fontaines--and from what you tell me, she might be casting the net to catch another fish."

The waiter shows up at the right time. I don't think Thomas could survive another minute without ordering a cold Abita. Not because he is thirsty, but because he's desperate for something to steady his nerves. I can feel the gears grinding in his head, trying to figure out how he can help. I don't want him involved. It's way too dangerous. All I need from him is information: what her plan is, who the new mark might be. Then I'll hand it off to the right people and let them take it from there. No way I'm putting Thomas on a perilous path of emotional pain.

"I'll have the Crispy Shrimp Salad and a Cup of Creole Gumbo," I tell the waiter—and then, thinking of my empty stomach, "Scratch that. Make it a bowl."

"I'll have the Blackened Chicken Salad. And a shot of Louisiana Tradition Bourbon," Thomas says with conviction.

A salad and a shot of Bourbon before noon? This news is hitting him hard.

"Don't give me that look, I'm pacing myself—for a towering slice of Chocolate Mousse Cake... and possibly a second Bourbon. Another perk of being your own boss: you can drink before noon without anyone writing you up."

"No judgment from me."

"I may even take the rest of the day off to steady my nerves," Thomas adds. "It's not every day you come face to face with a multiple murderer. You mentioned there were at least two dead men tied to her, right?"

"Two that we know of, there may be more," I say regrettably. Less is more here. And for once, I intend to follow that advice. I must remember I'm not addressing a forensic team, where disclosing all pertinent data is necessary for the resolution of a case.

"From what I read, three would officially make her a serial killer," Thomas says. "Oh my. Hearing myself say that out loud just made it worse."

"Thomas, you don't need to panic. You're just providing a service. There is no reason why she would harm you. She needs you to get that boat."

"I can't, in all good conscience," he says, squaring his shoulders. "What if Janet kills someone aboard? I can't be a part of that."

He's right. And seeing Thomas like this makes me want to protect him even more.

"I'll tell her the yacht company overbooked and her rental's not available," he says. "Then I'll close up shop and visit my family in Florida. For a very long, extended visit."

The food arrives just in time. We need a breather before diving back into the nightmare.

I don't want to push him, but I need something conclusive to pass on to Special Agent Larson. At the same time, I can't interrogate him like a suspect. He'll panic and forget the pertinent details, the ones that could be the key to taking Jane down.

At least people don't get hitched overnight. Jane takes her time building the fantasy to snare her victims before she moves in for the kill. So, as long as we don't spook her, she might lead us to the demise of her deception. We have to be diligent and intelligent about it. Let's keep a cool head and eat the Gumbo while it's hot.

I take a breath, steady my voice, and say, "Tell me exactly what she said about the boat. Why did she want it? Did she mention who would be joining her on the yacht? Is there a special occasion? Once I have the information, I'll contact Larson and give her the intel. I know it's tempting to want to pursue it to the end and find justice. Sometimes there is no end. As hard as it may be, we must accept it. All we can do is pass the torch to those in charge, and they can run with it to the finish line. I keep reminding myself, daily. I'm not a cop. Just someone who can't walk away from the truth.

Chapter 31

Jane/Janet?

"I remember everything she said. It seemed like a romantic fairytale. I'm surprised she didn't start with Once Upon a Time..." Thomas says with a dream-like expression. Maybe it was the Bourbon talking.

"Go on, did she mention any names?"

"Oh, yes, another thing I couldn't forget—Murray MacGregor, a Scottish gentleman of a certain age, she met on a cruise. He is the proud owner of many moorlands where Black Face Scottish sheep graze as far as the eye can see. She also mentioned that he owns houses and other properties in England and France."

"So, a wealthy older man with an expandable income who an attractive young lass can easily lure. It does have the makings for something sinister, given her track record. Now, why the yacht rental?"

"The way she put it was that she really liked him and wanted to impress him. She knew he was wealthy and didn't want him to think she was a gold digger. By inviting him to "Her" yacht, he would see that she had disposable income and had nothing to worry about."

"Well, that fits her M.O., except if you have to clarify that you're not a 'Gold-digger,' it stands to reason that you're probably one."

"She made it seem like she was looking out for the old lad, but I think she's looking for his old wallet," Thomas says, laughing at his little pun.

"Did you get any information as to where she's staying? Did she put a deposit down, and you wrote the information on a receipt?" I ask casually so as not to offend him if he didn't.

"I'll do you one better. I have all the information here or on my trusty phone." He smiles and scrolls away. "Here it is: She's staying at a friend's house on 3901 Louisa Street, New Orleans."

"That can't be."

"Why?"

"I've driven by there, and it's a large vacant lot, with a Huge sign with the number 3901 on a sign posted on the chain link fence. It sets across for the Regional Transit Authority. The last time I drove by, it had a few 18-wheelers scattered across the area. Unless she's staying in one of those, she deceived you with her address. Did the deposit go through to your bank account?"

"You know what, as you know, you came by shortly after she left the shop, so I didn't have time to check. At the time, I had no reason to be suspicious. Now, I'm panicked. What if she drained my account? Oh my."

"Take a breath. Jane, Janet, or whatever her name is, wouldn't rip you off, not at this point. She needs the boat. Afterward, I wouldn't give her access to your account. Who knows what tactics she may have to drain your account in one way or another? "She is untrustworthy and does not want to be found."

"So, no lead to speak of. Nothing worth anything to pass on?" He says, taking a long sip and signaling for another.

"Check your account. If that deposit is there, that may be a way to track her down. That's not up to us, but something Larson may have a way and a means to do."

"Keep your fingers crossed. I'm so nervous I can't even remember my password." His hand is shaking as he types on the screen. "Okay, I'm in. Here it is: $20,000 from some unpronounceable LLC. I hope this is enough."

"Thomas, I think it's time you go back to the shop, or better yet, go home and relax. I'll call Special Agent Larson; give her all the information you shared with me, and see what she does with it. I'll have her call you about the possible tracing of the banking account. Let's hope it can help trace her financials or whatever they need. After all, that's above my pay grade.

"Anything is better than nothing; one step closer to getting the run-away-bride to stop running."

Chapter 32

Shared-Intel

"Larson," her voice loud, clear, and full of confidence, answers the phone.

"Martin, here." Two can play that game. "I found her, well, I saw her, I followed her, then I lost her, but I learned about her next mark."

"Wait a minute, what do you mean, you followed her? She's not working alone; she and her pals are dangerous. What were you thinking?"

"I was thinking that I had to do something when she appeared at the coffee shop where I was meeting with a client. We made eye contact, and reaction time didn't leave me a choice. She didn't know I followed her. She had no idea. If I can sneak up on a wild boar and take pictures, I can definitely tail a self-indulgent woman who has crime on her mind."

Larson exhales loudly on the phone and starts drilling questions. After concisely giving her the lowdown on events and everything that Thomas had shared, she actually thanked me for the information—and then proceeded to scold me, telling me to leave the investigation to the professionals and stay out of the way. She softened her approach slightly when she added that she didn't want to see me hurt. If I did get hurt, she knew Robert would never let her live it down. Well, isn't that sweet? But she doesn't know me well enough to know that it is not a deterrent. My loyalty lies with the Fontaine family. I will do whatever it takes to make sure they come through this tragedy as well as they can. Emotionally, it will be a challenge, especially for Ethan. But eventually, they'll recover. So far, nobody has gotten hurt, and I intend to keep it that way.

"This is more than just about the money for her. It's the conquest of the game." Larson says as if thinking out loud.

"What do you mean?"

"We got a ransom call about an hour ago. We're setting up the drop of the money, getting everybody in place to hopefully take them down."

"Wait a minute, if you get the people that go for the money, there is a chance she won't be there. They don't usually do an exchange in plain sight with the kidnapped victim ready to walk towards the extorted parties. So even if you nail the guy or guys with their hands on the goody bag, they can still deny any knowledge of Jane and of working with her."

"That's true; after all, we know she's not going to return to the Fontaines and continue with the nuptials."

"We need to make sure she's the one implicated as the leader of the hoax, the one calling the shots, or else we have nothing. I'm sorry, I'm overstepping. I'm not trying to tell you how to do your job. I'm just eager to nail her before she gets away with it, free and easy and unto another mark." I say, backing down a bit on my assertive tone.

"No worries, I consider you one of the team. You've been working with and around law enforcement long enough to have your insight and intuition."

Part of the team. Great, this is the time to share my theory on how to proceed and ensure we nail Jane, Janet, or whatever her name is this week. We must come up with a nickname that encompasses all her personas.

"I have an idea. How about if we set up a stakeout at NOLA's Tourist Tours? Thomas could be a great help with a little prompting. He could call her and tell her to come down to the shop to sign some paper he forgot to give her for the yacht rental, once she shows up. Voila! You got her."

"I'll talk to the team and coordinate the setup. There can't be loose ends, and we don't want to get a civilian hurt."

"You're right. We don't want Thomas caught in the middle-- again.

Chapter 33

Unexpected Call

I needed to debrief. It's been over two hours since I sat here on the steps overlooking the grand Mississippi River. My coffee, which I picked up at Café du Monde, a block away, is still half full and cold. How is it that an event that seemed so right can turn into something so wrong? I've been away from my furry duo long enough for one day. The Sun is setting. Time to go. I'd better walk back to the car while enjoying the exuberant energy of the vendors and tourists alike who gather at and around Jackson Square.

For the time being, I should concentrate on my work, resetting the meeting with Evette Larue, and hope I haven't burned that bridge. I must stop chasing a case that isn't mine to chase. As Lora said, leave it to the professionals and let them figure it out. They have the means, the methods, and the mindset.

Finally, I made it to my ride, just as I left it this morning. That is a welcome sight. I don't need any more headaches. It's been a day; it feels like a week. I can't wait to get home to TK and TC and feel the unconditional love they always share from the moment I open the door.

Mommy is home! I don't need to announce myself, as TK is already jumping up and spinning her tail like a helicopter propeller. Meanwhile, TC remains on her perch atop the couch. She lifts her head, gives me a drowsy look, asserts that all is well, and goes back to sleep. I'm sure she'll wake up as soon as she hears her bowl filled with her favorite Keeble.

It's times like this, I wish I were a cat. Well, an indoor cat. One with good pet parents who provide all the necessities and ensure they stay indoors comfortably, avoiding becoming gator bait. The Bayou and its surrounding areas are not suitable for domesticated animals.

I'm all set for a quiet evening. Fortunately, I had some Creole Jambalaya leftovers, and that's a dish that's easy to reheat and enjoy. Of course, no microwave for me. I prefer my pan on the stove; that way, I can add a little more spice if so desired and inhale the savory scent that invigorates my appetite. That, paired with a nice glass of Bordeaux, will do the trick.

Wow, how's this possible? This Jambalaya tastes better than when I had it at the restaurant. It may be the company I'm keeping. Of course, I can't give any of this to TK or TC; it may be a little bit too spicy for them. Besides, I took care of feeding them before I sat down to eat. That way, they can't give me that, but mom, I'm starving. Look, that is so adorable, but a little too needy for my taste.

Let's see what's playing on TV; I'll go for a comedy. I'm burned out with mysteries at the moment. I want to sit, eat, watch, and drift into a restful sleep soon. Tomorrow will bring its own set of challenges. Therefore, there is no need to anticipate and worry about anything. I'm giving myself the night off.

Is it really 1 am? I question as I pick up my ringing phone, wondering who would be calling at this time of the night. After all, as the saying goes, nothing good happens after midnight. Now, that saying did not evolve here in NOLA, where the party life goes till the wee hours of the morning.

"Hello. Hello?" I repeat and clear my throat at the same time. I sense there is somebody on the line, but they're not talking. "Hello!" I almost shout into the phone.

"I'm sorry to call at this time, Jessica. This is Ethan. I need to talk with you."

"Ethan, what's going on?" I question. My heart is waking up and racing.

"I saw her...I saw her in the French Quarter." He says and breaks into sobs.

"Breathe, calm down, I'm here for you."

"I know, that's why I called you."

"Okay, let's start from the beginning; where did you see her, when did you see her, and what were you doing in the French Quarter this time of night?"

"I couldn't stand being home, with all the Feds, sitting around, waiting for a call, waiting for something to happen. I still don't believe that she is evil. I am sure there is an explanation. If I could talk with her."

"Okay, so you went out. Are you alone?" I ask, as he seems a bit intoxicated by his emotional state of denial.

"I'm with a couple of buddies, don't worry, Jess. I'm not driving. I always have a Big D whenever we go out. We take turns. Tonight was my night to have maybe one too many, but I can assure you, I saw her."

"Did any of your friends see her too?"

"By the time I realized it was her, and I got their attention as we were walking on Bourbon St., she had vanished."

Yeah, she's good at that, I say to myself, without letting on that I know how that is. I do not want to share that she's well, alive, and in the process of scamming somebody else. The last thing I want Ethan to do is go on a dragnet through the Quarter, trying to find her. This scenario is not Mission Impossible, and he's not Ethan Hunt."

"I would suggest that you safely find your way home. Give Special Agent Larson the details. Tell her what she was wearing when you saw her. Was it a disguise, a wig perhaps, or did she look like her normal self? They can ascertain camera footage and follow through. Maybe even find where she's hiding out. Did she seem to be by herself? Don't leave out any details. Everything and anything can lead to finding her. Perhaps once we find her, you may have the opportunity to discover the why. It may give you closure and help you move on."

"Can you help?" He says in desperation, voice quivering.

My heart breaks as I answer, "Ethan, I'm not police. There is only so much I can do. I don't have the assets law enforcement has to track people. However, I can assure you I'll do my best if or when I'm needed.

"Ehan, get home safe. I'll check on you tomorrow. Actually, later today, much later. Get some rest."

No rest for me; I will be contacting Larson in the morning, making sure he's taken seriously and not dismissed because of his intoxicated condition or the hangover he may experience in the early hours of the day.

Interestingly, I fell asleep while watching a comedy and woke up to a mystery again.

Was it really Jane he saw?

Chapter 34

The One AM Call

"Good morning, Jessica," Larson answers the phone in an unpredictably cheery tone. So, she has me on her phone; I am flattered.

"Good morning. Have you spoken to Ethan?"

"Well, yes and no. Ethan was talking this morning, but it wasn't making any sense. He mentioned he saw Jane, but he was all over the place. I told him to go back to bed, and we would discuss it later."

"The reason I'm calling is that he called me at one am, and he was certain that he saw Jane, but no sooner than he saw her when he tried to get his buddy's attention, she was gone."

"I don't mean to put my nose where it doesn't belong, but can you tell me what's going on? Have you made any progress? Ethan seemed frustrated and anxious; that's why he said he had to go out and blow up some steam."

"Well, we had to change tactics. The call came with ransom demands; they also stated that they would not negotiate as long as the Feds were involved. And things were starting to look dim for the bride if we didn't listen. We know she's not in danger, and she is the one orchestrating the whole thing, but we have to play along to get to her."

"So, what did you do? I ask, taking a long sip of my ice-cold lemonade.

"We left the premises; we got in our vehicles and drove away. It was brought to our attention by Stephan, the head of security, that their surveillance system was compromised. They were watching our every move. We had to make it look like we were leaving the Fontaines on their own."

"And you got back under the cloak of darkness? But how?" I say, using my Spidey senses.

"The cameras facing the Bayou lagoon in the back of the property were not compromised. We were able to turn them off without alerting them. We came back in the still of the night, under total blackout, using an electric boat, keeping the noise to a minimum. We used radar navigation and night vision goggles in total stealth mode."

"I'm impressed. So what now?" I ask.

"We'll talk to Ethan and see if he can give us something solid to follow. Location, and then we can coordinate with the cameras in the area and see if we can find a trail that will lead us to her whereabouts. I think our boy has got enough sleep. Anne is taking a fresh cup of extra-strong coffee to bring him back to life and get some intel we can use."

"Okay, I'll leave you to it; keep me posted. And stay invisible." I say, chuckling.

Now what? I just hung up, and Lora is calling. A call this soon, it can't be good.

"Ethan is not in his room; he's not in the house. His car is gone. And he's not answering his phone. It goes straight to voicemail."

"Can you still track him?"

"That will be a no... since he left it behind in his room."

"Well, he couldn't have left too long ago. And he would have been seen leaving on the cameras."

"We're looking into that, of course. But we can't give chase, as the perps would know we're still here. We'll have to utilize the security team. Maybe he's at a friend's house, staying away from the house for a bit. He is acting irresponsibly and complicating things. I'm not happy. Not happy at all."

So much for the cheery tone she had when we first spoke today. Now, where is Ethan? Where did he go?

Time to get to work. It will serve me well to visit Evette Larue. I'm hoping I'll catch her at her beloved supposed-to-be-haunted mansion. After all, she wanted me to do a trial photoshoot to see if my photographic vision matches hers. It will be one way to make up for my impromptu exit the other day. I won't charge her. Hopefully, she'll be pleased, and I'll be able to land the assignment. Sometimes, one has to go the extra mile to make life worthwhile.

This area can't be the right place. It seems like an industrial area. It is not what you would expect surrounding a plantation house built in the late 1700s. According to my GPS, I'm on the right street. Sanctuary Drive, I'm passing a nondescript beige building, which is the New Orleans Police Department. And wow, here is the LeFuffe Plantation. As if transported in time, surrounded by an unassuming low white fence. It does have an electric gate with a call box, but for some reason, I expected a large fortress-type fence. The green lawn spreads out and surrounds the mansion, with various ancient trees overhanging. The house discreetly peeks through the greenery, as if watching the guests as they dare to visit. It is a stark contrast to the surrounding area. I'll park outside the gate, announce myself, and walk up the long path. Two reasons: one, I need to get in my steps, and second, I don't want to get trapped inside the gates just in case there's an angry ghost on the property, or a power failure. I can hop over this fence if need be. Let's hope it doesn't come to that. Perhaps I've watched too many horror movies, but you can never be too careful.

I hope she's in. Final thoughts before pressing the button on the intercom box. Why is it that no matter how lightly one presses the button, it still sounds overly loud and annoying? Is it that obnoxious inside the house? And there it is, the camera on top of the gate post. Do I look camera-ready?

"Alo' Jessica, let me fuzz you in. You have no car?"

"I think walking in will give me a better feel of the place if you don't mind."

"But, of course, whatever you think is best. I'll get some cool lemonade ready."

"See you in a few." Is walking really what I want to do in this humid heat? I'm committed now, as I mentioned, to getting a feel for the place. What was I thinking? My shirt is already sticking to my back. This visit may not be a fantastic second impression. I'd better get my camera ready and start snapping pictures. I must wow her with my photographic creative edge, and maybe my lens will capture something surreal that will sell her on hiring me.

"Come in, please. You're a real trooper. I can't believe you walked in this heat. The house is as authentic to the era as possible, but discreetly, we installed two air conditioners. That way, our visitors are comfortable when they come through. The chill in the air does help create a haunted house atmosphere. Nes pas?

"I took some pictures of the exterior just to show you some angles that make it interesting and foreboding. I also used a special lens with darkening effects. Even though the photos taken are in bright daylight, it looks like dusk."

"I do like that, C'est bon. You don't have to convince me anymore. I appreciate your dedication and innovative thinking. You have the job. This check is a deposit, and then when we choose all the shots, I pay the rest. Yes?"

As I glance at the check, I'd be a fool to say no—so I say, "YES, Merci!"

"Now, let's sit for a bit, have something cold, and then I'll show you around the house."

"Do you live here?"

"Oh no, mon Cher. I would not stay here overnight. No way. I make sure I leave and go home before sundown. I live just outside the Quarter."

"So, there is more than just rumors?"

"Another day, I will tell you the true history of this place. Now, let me show you around, and then we'll head out to celebrate with a lovely meal in the Quarter. Se bien?

Chapter 35

A Peaceful Lunch

"It must be our lucky day, finding two parking spaces on St. Ann Street," I say to Evette as she climbs out of her car, which is parked right in front of mine.

"This place is worth the walk, even if you have to park a few blocks away. Have you been?"

"No, not yet, though I've heard wonderful things—food, décor, ambiance. And, of course, the history."

"Muriel's Jackson Square is one of my favorites," she says, looping her arm through mine in that charming European way.

For a moment, I feel like I've stumbled into friendship, the real kind. When Evette isn't wearing her business armor, she's warm, easy to admire. I envy her ability just to be present. I'm more like a dog with a bone: once I latch onto something, I gnaw it until it's resolved or gone. But tonight, I decide to follow her lead—no ghosts to chase, no puzzles to solve—just a good meal.

"Here we are," she says as we step inside. "Take a breath—this is the best of the best in Original Creole cuisine. Sometimes it's almost too much for the senses. That's why I have my favorite table on the balcony. Perfect for people-watching."

"That sounds fantastic."

She waves to the host, who lights up at the sight of her. She's clearly a regular.

"Pierre, how have you been? I missed you last time."

"I just came back from a trip home to Paris," Pierre says, his accent wrapping around every syllable. "One must visit the family, n'est-ce pas? And who is this lovely lady?"

"But of course—this is Jessica Martin. She's an out-standing photographer. She'll be shooting all my Mason photos. If you need new pictures for the restaurant, I highly recommend her."

I'm stunned by her gracious introduction, but I extend my hand. Pierre bows and lifts it to his lips. I nearly giggle like a teenager, but swallow it back and smile, resisting the urge to curtsy.

"This is gorgeous," I say as we settle at the table, overlooking Jackson Square lit up in the golden hour glow.

"I thought you'd enjoy it," Evette says. "For this view, the weather has to cooperate, and tonight is perfect, not too hot, low humidity. You can't do better."

"This is as perfect as it gets. Thank you for sharing it with me. In this town, there are so many amazing places to eat that if I lived a hundred years, I'd never get to them all."

"That's true, but once you find what you love, you stick to it. And I love this place. The food is grand, and the service is better. Now, what will you have? Order anything you like—tonight we celebrate creative partnerships." She waves over the waiter, who practically sprints to the table. "Bring us a bottle of the Laurent-Perrier Harmony Champagne."

I could get used to clients like this—people who appreciate good work and have no qualms paying for it. Still, a pang of loss for Antoine DuBois catches me off guard. He'd been such a fighter over every invoice. Sometimes, money isn't everything. But sometimes, it sure doesn't hurt.

Champagne arrives, and we toast to new beginnings.

I'm savoring my first bite of shrimp and grits when my phone buzzes on the table. I should have silenced it. Then again, it's Larson.

"I'm sorry," I say to Evette as I stand. "I have to take this."

I walk to the far end of the balcony, away from diners. "Larson, what's going on?"

"We got into Ethan's phone. He texted her. She agreed to meet."

"Where?" My heart sinks. "Since he left the phone behind, I assume he didn't want anyone tracking him. What the heck was he thinking?"

"Clearly, he wasn't."

"Details—where are they meeting?"

"We have a team en route. Fifteen minutes out."

"Where, Larson?"

"Jackson Square. Corner of St. Ann and Chartres."

I turn, gripping the balcony rail. "I'm here. I'm literally across the street—I can see Ethan and What's her name."

"Don't intervene. We're on it. Just keep eyes on them and stay in contact."

"A white van just pulled up. It's in my line of sight. I'm going downstairs. If they move, I'm not losing them."

Another dinner abandoned. I jog back to the table, phone still pressed to my ear. "Evette, I'm so sorry. I have to go. I'll explain everything later. Merci. Bon appétit." Saying it in French doesn't make me feel any less awful. Twice now, I've left her sitting alone. That's no way to treat a client.

I hurry down the stairs, weaving through the tables, clearing my head. Focus. Eyes on them.

"They're still talking," I whisper. "I'm in the shadows—no way they'll see me. Darn that van. It's blocking half my view."

"Don't let them spot you," Larson murmurs.

"Relax. There's a vendor with a T-shirt stand and a tall mirror. Perfect cover."

I slip behind it and watch their reflection in the glass. The conversation is escalating—lots of hand-waving. Ethan is shaking his head, backing away. She's reaching for his arm. He pulls free.

"What's happening?" Larson demands.

"The van's reversing—wait. Two men, masks—oh, heck. They're going for him. She's holding his arm. Where are you?"

I shove the phone in my pocket and sprint across the pavement—no time to wait. Larson's voice crackles from inside my jacket, but I can't stop.

Ethan is fighting them, and I'm grateful he's strong enough to slow them down. I grab the top bar from the T-shirt display, yank it free, and charge.

I swing, cracking the bar across Jane's arms. She lets go. One of the masked men whirls around and lands a punch square on my nose. Pain explodes behind my eyes—hot, blinding. I stumble, vision blurred, but I see enough to spot the gun.

For a split second, I freeze. One of the men shoves a hood over Ethan's head. I launch forward anyway. My eyes are streaming. The gun barrel comes down, cracking against my forehead.

The world tilts. I hit the ground hard, blinking up at the blurry streetlights.

The last thing I see is the van roaring away down Chartres Street, Ethan inside.

I fight to stay conscious. Sirens wail in the distance. Larson's voice is still coming from my pocket—a small, tinny reassurance that I'm still alive.

People stand there, filming. Nobody helps.

Then, a pair of hands reaches down. A handkerchief presses against my bleeding nose. A stranger's voice asks gently, "Are you all right?"

Maybe the world isn't all bad after all.

Chapter 36

Déjà-Vu-ER Time

"I will not take no for an answer," Larson says firmly. "I told you to keep an eye on them. You did, and you got hurt—on my watch. You're riding in the ambulance to the hospital so doctors can check you out.

"Well, if you put it that way," I sigh. "I can assure you, I'm fine. Nothing an ice pack won't handle. But, okay. I get it—liability and all that."

"It goes beyond that." She rubs her forehead, looking tired for the first time tonight. "I actually like you. Not as much as Robert does—and he's part of the reason you need to get to the hospital. My butt's on the line when he hears you got hurt doing impromptu surveillance for me. I don't even know what I'm going to tell him. But there's going to be a lot of backpedaling involved. Now—" She gestures at the paramedics. "Listen to these gentlemen.

Let them check you out. I have serious regrouping to do. Now that we have a real kidnapping to supersede the fake kidnapping, I need to contact the Fontaines. Telling them their son was kidnapped practically under our noses, that's not going to be easy."

"I hope Ethan's okay," I say quietly. "Find him. Bring him home."

"I will. And you—take care of yourself." She squeezes my shoulder before turning away.

I'm not sure the lights and sirens were necessary, but Larson clearly made it non-negotiable. She even specified Ochsner Medical Center—only the best for the liability nightmare I've become.

It feels like déjà vu, rolling through the ER doors on a gurney. Last time, I came in with Robert and Clark, a neat little forehead gash. Now I'm sporting a bonus nose injury. Maybe they'll give me a two-for-one discount.

A nurse wheels me into a bay curtained off from the rest of the chaos. Moments later, a familiar face appears.

"Jessica—you're back," says Dr. Tran. "I'm not sure if you remember me."

"Of course I do." I manage a smile, though my nose chooses that exact moment to start bleeding again. Perfect. "You were very kind last time."

"Let's get you fixed up," he says briskly. "This is Jasmine—she'll help get you settled."

Jasmine gives me a warm smile. "We keep meeting like this, Miss Jessica."

"Lucky me," I say, pinching the bridge of my nose. "Though I'd prefer it under different circumstances."

"Don't you worry." She's already moving, gathering supplies, and sliding on gloves. "We'll have you cleaned up in no time."

"I really don't think all this is necessary," I protest as she hooks up an IV. "Just a little pressure on my nose, maybe some antiseptic—"

"Hon, I hate to disagree," she says gently, "but you're going to need stitches this time. You got away without them before, but you're not that lucky today."

I sigh. "Any other treatment options that don't involve needles in my forehead?"

"Yeah," Jasmine deadpans. "I suggest you wear a helmet from now on."

I roll my eyes, even as I grin. "I suggest you keep your day job."

Dr. Tran returns, snapping on a fresh pair of gloves. "Miss Martin, you're going to feel a little pressure."

Before I can ask what he means, he grips my nose and gives it a decisive tug. My vision goes white, and for one terrifying second, I think I'm going to pass out—but then, blessedly, I can breathe.

He nods, satisfied. "Good news—your nose will be swollen, but there's no septal hematoma."

"In English, please," I say, dabbing the tears from my eyes.

"No collection of blood inside the septum," he clarifies. "The swelling will go down in a few days, and the bruising will fade. No permanent damage."

I let out a shaky laugh. "So I'll still be able to smell the roses. Good. And the stitches?"

"We'll minimize scarring as much as possible," he says. "I've called in a colleague who specializes in plastics. After a month or so, you probably won't even see the scar."

"Honestly, it's fine. Worst case, I'll grow out bangs. And no concussion, right?"

"We checked—your pupils are normal, no headache, no confusion. You were very fortunate."

"Fortunate," I repeat, glancing down at my blood-speckled clothes. "Sure. Let's call it that."

He hesitates. "In your line of work...these things happen."

"My line of work?" I raise an eyebrow.

He looks a little embarrassed. "Well...law enforcement, right? Some capacity?"

I let out a soft laugh. "No. I'm a photographer. Law enforcement was a long time ago. Just a case of being in the wrong place at the wrong time."

"Oh." He clears his throat. "Well. I hope I don't see you back here anytime soon."

"Likewise, Doctor."

He gestures toward Jasmine. "She'll get you ready for Dr. Erik Manège. He'll take care of the stitches."

"Thank you," I say sincerely.

As he steps away, I can't help but think that if I do end up back here, they ought to name a bed after me.

Chapter 37

Rob The Bot

"Thanks for picking me up, Renee. I know I must be a sight."

"Not a problem, I've seen worse."

"That's not saying much. You work at a funeral home."

"I don't see you driving any time soon, so do I take you home, and then you can make arrangements to pick up your ride from the Quarter?"

"I'm not going to worry about that now. I want to go home. It's late, I'm tired, and I need to see my furry babies. It seems every day; I get less time with them. I'm afraid they're going to pack a bag and run away from home."

"You know, I'm curious as to how this happened to you. You tell me you're going to meet a new client. The one that you ran out of the other day in your first meeting. Then you end up in the hospital, I guess, she didn't buy your apologies. If I were you, I would think twice about working for somebody with such a temper."

"Renee, are you serious? My client didn't do this. I was with my client at Muriel's, having dinner. I'll give you the condensed version. Dinner had just been delivered to the table when Agent Larson called me about the Fontaines' case. Ethan took off and left his phone behind. Getting into his phone, they were able to get to his messages. They found out he was on his way to Jackson Square to meet the alleged kidnapped bride. Since we were on the balcony, I saw them. I went downstairs to stay close in case I had to follow them, Larson said, they were on their way."

"So, you were playing cop, yet again."

"No, not really. I was keeping an eye on them. Then a Van pulled up, and the back doors opened. She wouldn't let go of Ethan. Two guys in masks jumped out and tried to put a black bag over Ethan's head. He was putting up a good fight. I took the opportunity to assist, and the rest is written all over my face."

"So, you were not playing cop; you were playing cape Crusader without the cape."

"What would you have done, set there and watch them carry him off?"

"I may poke fun at you, but honestly, I'm proud of you. This world needs more people who will put themselves on the line to help others."

"You don't think I'm nuts for jumping in?"

"I may think you're insane from time to time; after all, you do tend to get into extreme situations. But I'm still proud. And I know if something happened to me, you'd have my back."

"That you can count on," I say, trying not to get misty.

"Oh my! There is your Jeep in the driveway. I didn't know the FBI, valet parks.

"Wait a minute, there is a black SUV parked across the street, and it looks occupied. Don't get out yet." I say, reaching out and preventing her from exiting the car.

"It's probably one of the Feds making sure you got home."

"I would think Larson would have called me to tell me they would bring my car."

"I think Larson has bigger fish to fry, with the kidnapping and all."

"We're staying put until they get out and show themselves."

"You can let go of my arm now. The door is opening, and that's definitely FBI. One tall FBI guy."

"Oh yeah, that's Agent Silent."

"What?"

"I've never heard him speak; he just nods. I think he's part AI. Maybe it's like a new defense prototype. Just don't stare."

I'll get out of the car and see what he has to say. If anything, at all. This exchange should be interesting. I'm glad he's on our side. He is truly menacing, especially in this low-light situation.

"Miss Martin, Agent Clark and I brought your car back. We didn't know when you would be able to arrange to pick it up, and we didn't think it would be safe to leave it on the street. From what I understand, there is street sweeping there tomorrow. We felt that you'd been through enough today and didn't need to get your car towed. I hope it is okay that one of our agents drove your vehicle."

"Well, thank you, thank you very much. By the way, where is Clark?" I'm hoping he's still not in the car, waiting for an invitation to get out.

"He had to run, so he took a ride back to head office—there is much to do in light of the new kidnapping."

"Yes, I can imagine. By the way, I never got your name."

"I'm Rob, Jayme Rob, Special Agent Rob." He says, making it very clear what his name is.

Of course, I cannot help myself when I ask. "Rob, is that short for something?"

"No, just Rob." He says without cracking a smile and continues without missing a beat, "We have checked out the premises, and everything is as it should be. Your dog and cat are very cute. One of them barks a lot; it is understood that he is watching the premises for your safety. Here are the keys to your vehicle. Nice ride."

"Thank you, Agent Rob. I appreciate it. My friend Renee and I are going to go in now. Have a good night."

"Yes, you too, Miss Martin."

"That dude is a little off. I'm not sure about the AI thing, but maybe special training—from another planet."

"Okay, enough already. I've had enough excitement for one day; I don't need to have nightmares thinking the FBI has robots or AI humanoids working for them or with them." I say, shaking, a shiver going down my back.

"Think about it...his name is R O B, as a 'Robot.'" Renee says and proceeds to sing the sound from the Twilight Zone.

"Could you make some Chamomile Tea, please? I'll check the answering machine. There are a ton of messages.

First message: Hi Jessica, this is Thomas. I tried your cell, but you weren't answering; you would know that. Anyway, I need you to call me.

Second message: Jessica is me, Thomas. Call me as soon as possible. It's about Janet; she wants to go to the Marina and see another boat. I need to know what to do. There is something fishy about it. No, I'm not trying to be funny--you know how I get when I'm nervous.

Third message: I'm worried I'm not reaching you. I'm at the Marina now. I have keys to a couple of boats. I wanted to humor her with her request. I don't want to say something that's going to upset her. Call me.

Fourth message: I met with her; she was looking at a 35-foot Cigarette boat. I guess she wants to take the Old guy on a wild ride. I don't know what she's thinking. She has a couple of guys with her. She said she needed a minute to discuss things with her colleagues. So I stepped away to call you. Something is not right.

Fifth message: I guess they like the red and white 35-footer. They're loading stuff on it. They're not supposed to do that. I'm not letting them take the boat at night. I have no paperwork from the owners. You know me, everything by the book. What do I do? Wait a minute, they're carrying somebody onto the boat. He doesn't seem to be well. Barely walking. I need you, Jess.

Sixth message: Jessica, I'm calling the police-- Come with us. Hang up the phone and come along. Give me the keys, I said, give me the keys. Don't you get smart? You throw the keys in the water; you're going in after them--

"He's in trouble, real trouble. I must call Larson now."

"When was the last call?" Renee asks as the kettle whistles in the kitchen. There is no time for tea.

"The last call came in about two hours ago. They could be anywhere by now."

Chapter 38

Thomas Taken

"Can't talk now. Thomas was taken," I blurt out as I answer Robert's call.

"You mean Ethan?"

"No, Thomas was grabbed at the marina. Ethan was kidnapped earlier at Jackson Square. I'll call you later—I have to reach Larson."

I hang up and punch in Larson's number, my heart hammering—no time to waste.

"Special Agent Lora Larson. Please leave a message at the beep, and I'll get back to you as soon as I can."

"Fantastic," I mutter. "Voicemail on the first ring—she must be on another call."

I pace, trying to think. "Who do I know who has a boat?"

"What are you planning?" Renee asks warily. "You're not seriously thinking about heading out into alligator-infested waters alone to chase kidnappers."

"They left from Seabrook Harbor on Lake Pontchartrain. If I had to bet, they're going to cut through Lake Borgne and out to the Gulf. We can't sit around; they'll probably demand ransom for Ethan, but Thomas doesn't have rich relatives. He's just a witness who got in the way."

"Wait—what about Jac? Thomas's friend with the boats?" Renee says, already pulling out her phone. "He helped before."

"Perfect. I'll call Jac."

As soon as he picks up, I don't waste breath. "Jac, it's Jessica—Thomas's friend. I need your help."

"What's going on?"

"Thomas was taken, probably aboard a red and white Cigarette boat out of Seabrook. I need to track it and find them. He's in real danger."

"Get over here," Jac says without hesitation. "I'll call my buddy at the marina. Most of those high-end boats have trackers. We'll figure it out. You called the police yet?"

"I'm... working with them, but there's too much red tape. Thomas is my responsibility. I can't let anything happen to him."

"Understood. Just get here."

Renee crosses her arms, giving me that squinty look that means she's officially unimpressed. "Jessica, call Larson again. You can't go rogue."

"I'll call her on the way," I say, grabbing my jacket and shoving my phone into my back pocket. "By then, I'll have something solid, coordinates, a plan. You know my rule: it's better to ask for forgiveness than permission."

"Wait—I'm coming too."

"No. If something happens, you know who I'm with and what we were doing. Do me a favor—take care of my babies."

Driving to Jac's place, I'm weighing how much to share with Larson. Part of me hopes she won't pick up until I can pin down exactly where the boat's heading. But if she calls back, I won't have the luxury of stalling.

Come on. Pick up. Pick up.

"Special Agent Lora Larson—"

Voicemail again. I leave a quick message and hang up before I can second-guess myself.

By the time I pull up, Jac is already waiting at the dock, flashlight in hand.

"Jessica, you made it in record time," he calls. "Are you sure you're up to this?" He asks as I step into the light, which reveals my bruised face and bandaged head, covertly covered under my baseball cap.

"I am fine, it's just superficial."

"Okay, if you say so. Put on a life jacket. I've got intel you'll want to hear."

"Don't keep me in suspense."

"You were right—there's a tracker. The coordinates put them here—" He squints at his phone, the screen glowing in the dark. "Thirty point two-zero-seven-eight-one latitude, eighty-nine point one-zero-six-seven-five longitude."

I take a breath. "I don't have my nautical charts—where is that, exactly?"

"Smugglers Cove. Mississippi side. Only accessible by private boat. It'll take us at least a couple of hours—maybe longer. They've got a lead."

"Smugglers Cove," I repeat. "By Cat Island. I know the area. I did a photoshoot for a realtor there. They almost sold one of the houses. The family changed their mind and decided to keep it as a vacation getaway. It's vacant most of the time."

"Then you know how isolated it is," Jac says, serious now. "This girl's fast," he pats the hull, "but not Cigarette-boat fast. They're probably ignoring the speed limit. I can't. I'll lose my license."

"Then we need to leave. Now."

"I'm ready," he says, gesturing to a cooler. "Water, snacks. Everything we need."

I glance at him—and spot the holster under his jacket. "Is that what I think it is?"

"Open carry. We don't know who we're up against. But we know the bad guys do."

"True dat," I say, forcing a grin. I can't afford fear.

He nods at a duffel bag tucked under a seat. "Check that."

Inside: two pairs of night-vision goggles, a hatchet, a flare gun, spare flares, a first aid kit which includes a snake and insect bite kit, zip ties, a survival knife with a compass, a machete, and a taser. I zip it shut, feeling oddly steadied. This is no impulsive stunt; this is a mission.

Jac unties the bow line. I grab the stern. "Midnight run," I murmur.

"Under the cover of darkness," he agrees. "No flashlights. No noise."

"We'll get there."

He looks at me, and for a second, we share the same thought: failure isn't an option.

The engine rumbles to life. I glance back at the lights onshore, a silent promise forming in my chest. Hang on, Thomas. We're coming for you.

Chapter 39

SEAL To The Rescue

It feels like the calm before the storm. Riding the water with nothing but the engine slicing through the dark is almost hypnotic. Glancing at Jac—without being creepy—gives me a strange comfort. His steady gaze locked on the inky horizon shows a determination I can't help but trust. Who is this man, really? More than a Bayou dweller with a rental business, that much is clear.

I have two hours to decide if he'll risk everything to keep me alive. Usually, trust builds over countless hours of small talk and shared routine. Not tonight. Tonight, he's my partner, and I have to believe he's as committed as I am. When I commit, I'm all in. No exceptions.

"So Jac, what's your story?"

"My story? Not much of one. Some doors close, others open. When they do, you step through and keep going."

"Wow, could you be more cryptic? We've got a couple of hours to kill, and you're giving me the mysterious Lone Wolf routine. Look, you don't know me, except that I'd risk everything for Thomas. I need to know you'll have my six when it counts."

"I thought you were just a photographer. But the way you speak—and handle yourself, injuries and all—it tells me there's more behind the lens."

"Okay, that's how you're going to play it? I'll go first. Before I came back to New Orleans to be a commercial photographer, I worked in Los Angeles as a forensic photographer. What drew me in was that, right after graduating from the police academy, I realized I could capture details that others overlooked. My sergeant saw the potential and had me shadow the senior forensic photographer whenever there was a case. And in LA, there's always a case.

I still went on calls as an officer and even helped with homicide when they needed it. But my creative streak—and my puzzle-solving mind—pulled me toward forensics full time. I still have the training. Maybe it's a little rusty, but the knowledge, tactics, and emotional control are all still with me."

"I guess it's my turn. I don't like to talk about my past, but in this case, I feel I must."

"As long as you don't have to take me out to silence me after you tell me—go ahead."

Jac takes a deep breath. Even now, this clearly still hurts him.

"I was a Navy SEAL."

"I can see that. You're ready for anything. Or is that just what you tell the ladies over a few drinks?" I try to defuse the heaviness hanging between us.

"It's not something I usually mention or like to think about. But you opened up, so it's only fair I do the same if we're in this together."

"Ready when you are," I say, quieter now.

"There's not much to say." He stares into the darkness over the water. "I was a SEAL. I loved it. We were on a retrieval mission off the Florida coast—six of us on the dive. My partner got his gear caught in some debris. He was a few feet behind me. When I realized, I went back to help."

He pauses, and I stay silent.

"It took longer than I thought to free him. We were running low on air. For some reason, our comms with the ship failed. He made it to the surface safely, but I was already almost out of oxygen. I shot up too fast."

"The Bends?" I ask.

He nods. "Decompression Illness. It nearly killed me. I recovered eventually, but I couldn't dive as I had before. They offered me reassignment, a way to stay in. But I couldn't do it. I was either all in or out."

He looks over at me, and there's a softness in his eyes.

"I chose out, away from all of it. I got an honorable discharge. The higher-ups said, I saved my buddy's life, so I guess it was worth it. If I had to do it over again, I wouldn't change a thing."

He cracks the faintest smile.

"After all, we lived to tell the tale—even if it takes someone poking it out of me."

"Would you like something to drink?" I ask, trying to diffuse the heaviness of what he just shared.

"I wouldn't say no to a brandy, but I'll settle for water," he says, straightening his shoulders and shedding some of the tension.

"Coming right up, my Captain." I chuckle, feeling an unexpected sense of camaraderie.

"Let's implement the One-Second Decision. SEALs swear by it."

"I'm not familiar with that one, but if it's good enough for the SEALs, I won't argue."

"The One-Second Decision is about not giving in to impulses or emotional reactions. You take one second to regain control of your thoughts and choose a deliberate, rational response—one based on what you really want, not just this moment."

"So, I take it we'll be discussing strategy—how we're going to approach, how to figure out which house they're in, and how to breach."

"No offense, but you're getting a bit ahead of yourself. Maybe we should contact the agent in charge and loop her in before we charge into anything."

"You're right. For a minute, I forgot about the Feds and their protocol."

"I'm sure the agent—Larson.—will appreciate having you as an asset. But she won't appreciate you going rogue."

"You're the second person who's said that to me today. I don't know why everyone assumes that."

"If the shoe fits."

"Look, I'm calling Special Agent Larson, okay?"

"You don't have to go exactly by the book—just stick to a few pages." He laughs at his own wit.

"I don't have service. Not even a single bar. Do you?"

"I have something better. A satellite phone." He reaches into a compartment and hands it to me.

"Of course, you have a satellite phone. Do you also have a pen that shoots darts?"

"I was a SEAL, not James Bond."

I grin and hit the call button. "Larson, can you hear me?"

"Yes, Jessica, I hear you loud and clear. Where are you?"

"I'm on a boat."

"What are you doing on a boat? Don't tell me you're out there giving chase to the kidnappers."

"No, of course not. They're long gone. We—as in Jac and I—are on our way to Smuggler's Cove. He's a former

Navy SEAL, so you have nothing to worry about. According to intel we gathered from the marina, the GPS shows the boat near Cat Island."

"We finally got the GPS coordinates. There was nobody at the marina when we arrived, so it took time to track down the records. How did you get them so fast?"

"Jac is friends with the head guy at the marina. Had his cell number. It's a done deal—we know where they are, and that's where we're going."

"You can't go there by yourselves. We're ready to head out. We'll be there in a few hours."

"And we'll be there in less than half an hour. We need to scout the houses on the island and figure out where they're holding them."

"Don't do anything more. I forbid it. This is an order—stand down."

"Sorry, you're breaking up. I lo—" I say, then conveniently kill the connection.

"You are incorrigible," Jac says, shaking his head. "You just ignored a direct command from a Special Agent of the FBI."

"It does sound that way," I admit, unable to hide my grin. "But it's the intention that counts. Besides, I'm just a civilian trying to help a friend out. Right?"

Chapter 40

No Time To Wait

On approach, the island is silent and desolate. Did the GPS give us the wrong coordinates? No lights flicker from the moonlit silhouettes of the houses.

With the engine raised out of the water, we have no choice but to use the oars to creep forward. The air smells of brine and rotting vegetation, thick enough to taste. My head throbs under the pressure of the night vision gear pressing against my bandaged forehead. But I don't have an alternative. Without the goggles, there's not enough light to avoid the snags—half-submerged trees and the sharp intrusions jutting out of the marsh.

Besides, I'm sitting next to a former SEAL. No way am I going to complain and get myself demoted to the rank of Guppy.

We follow a narrow, finger-like waterway that soon dead-ends. The boat could stay here, but come daylight, it will be exposed to anyone watching from the point.

Jac catches my eye. He lifts a flat hand—Stop. Then two fingers point to his eyes and sweep toward the north shore—Look there.

I nod, feeling a mosquito land on my cheek. I fight the instinct to slap it away. If this is the price of stealth, so be it.

We silently agree to turn around. Jac curls two fingers toward his chest—Back out. I ease my oar into the water, every movement measured, deliberate.

I rack my memory for details. The second house has a small beach, a dock for its own boat, and easier access. More importantly, it's shaded by a thick canopy of trees stretching all the way to the porch. If we're going to get in without being seen, that's our best bet.

The silence between us is absolute. Communication comes down to a glance, a nod, a quick hand gesture—Hold position, Proceed slowly, Eyes up. The only sounds are the frogs, the buzzing insects, and my pulse pounding in my ears like a war drum.

Somewhere behind us, something splashes into the water. Too big to be a frog.

Just as I feared, they've taken over the Reyes family house—the vacation place the owners only used a few times a year.

There are two boats tied to the dock. One looks like an eighteen-foot Chris-Craft, the other unmistakably the red and white Cigarette boat.

I only hope Jane and her crew didn't hurt the Reyes family. Maybe they broke in because it was empty—just another crime of opportunity, one they'd obviously planned.

We haul the boat onto the sandy embankment, easing it up the shore until it grinds to a stop with a low scrape. Before we disembark, we scan the area—watching for anything with claws, fangs, or a trigger finger. The air is thick with salt and decay, every sound carrying sharply across the water.

Jac unzips a duffel and pulls out two waters, a bag of chips, a protein bar, and a few folded articles. From another duffel, he retrieves a tactical vest, straps it on, and slips a pack over his shoulders. His movements are methodical, silent, like he's done this a hundred times.

I almost ask about the snacks, but I keep my mouth shut. There's always a reason, and this isn't a photo safari. I know when to follow.

He points to the gear and says, "Take whatever you're comfortable with. Leave the rest."

Before we leave the boat behind, we break some branches as silently as we can, pick some others already on the ground, and cover the vessel for additional camouflage.

Then he gives me a thumbs-up—clear. He taps his chest, then gestures to the smaller outbuilding near the tree line. I nod, feeling a thread of relief cut through the nerves. He's taking point, precisely as he should.

The shed could be empty. Or it could be a holding place. If the hostages are in there, it'd be a miracle. We could cut them loose, sprint back to the boat, and disappear before anyone realized we'd ever been here. But nothing ever goes that clean.

I clip the knife to my belt on the right and let the machete hang at my left hip. With all this scrub and undergrowth, it might earn its keep soon enough.

Jac signals again—two fingers to his eyes, then a sweeping motion toward the main house. Watch for movement. My heart picks up speed, hammering against my ribs.

I slip around the back of the shed, crouched low. It smells like mildew and rust. A broken rake leans against the doorway. I ease the door open a few inches. Inside, only darkness and the stale air of a space long abandoned. No voices. No sign of life.

I rejoin Jac near the edge of the trees. From here, we can see the main house in full view. All the upstairs rooms are dark. Only two pools of light were glowing, spilling across the back porch, the other a softer amber behind the big window near the front door. The living room, maybe.

Jac lowers himself into a crouch and signals again—flat hand out: hold position. Then a quick flick of two fingers to his eyes—keep watch.

We're not here to play heroes. Not yet. Our job is to confirm they're here, count how many people we're dealing with, and get out before anyone knows we were close.

I keep my eyes trained on the windows, every muscle wound tight. Shadows drift across the curtain in the front room—someone's moving around in there.

If we're lucky, we have a few more hours of darkness before dawn starts peeling back our cover.

We'll gather every scrap of intel we can, slip back to the boat, and send it all to Larson. Then we wait.

The wait is the part most people can't stand—the stillness before everything breaks loose.

If I'm reading Jac's signals right, he's going to move closer to the house and check things out. He wants me to pull back to the boat. I hate this. I wish we had comms—earbuds, anything—so we could at least whisper. But if we can't talk, we can't argue. Fine. I'll be good. I'll obey orders and retreat for now.

How long will it take Larson to get here? Will they come in stealthily, or will helicopters flood the island with the Night Sun, announcing the end of the line for everyone inside?

Meanwhile, I sit here, providing a buffet for the mosquitoes. I know I forgot something—good mosquito repellent. Maybe Jac has some stashed in the boat. He seems to have thought of everything else.

A faint thump breaks the monotony. I scan the dark but see nothing. I slip the goggles back on, ignoring how they dig into my forehead.

Another thump—louder this time.

Oh God. It's Thomas.

He's running in blind panic, stumbling through the yard, getting up, and sprinting again. This is bad—he's going to bolt straight into the marsh.

I have to decide to run for the house to alert Jac, or chase Thomas before he disappears into the dark.

No time to hesitate. I go after Thomas.

With the goggles, I have the advantage—I can see where I'm going. Tread lightly. Don't fall, I remind myself.

He runs fast for someone in loafers. It's amazing what pure terror can do for speed.

I'm gaining on him. He keeps thrashing forward, probably thinking I'm one of the kidnappers.

How far from the house do I need to be before I can risk calling out? I don't have a choice. If I don't stop him, he's liable to run straight into an alligator's jaws.

"Thomas! Thomas, it's me—Jess! Stop running!"

I think he heard; maybe he's finally running out of steam. The night goes unsettlingly still, as if even the frogs are waiting.

"Thomas, where are you? Answer me! It's Jessica. If you can hear me, tap on something—anything."

A faint tapping comes from ahead. I follow the sound.

Branches crackle underfoot—another tap. Then I see him.

"Thomas, I'm here. You're okay. I'll get you out."

"Jessica—is that you? I'm stuck."

"Yes. It's not quicksand—it's just a branch caught on your belt."

"But I'm in the mud."

"You are. But it's not like the movies—you won't get sucked under. Hold still."

I circle and free him.

"Oh Jess, I'm so glad to see you. I thought we were finished."

"How did you escape?"

"Well, so far, they've been...polite. I guess I'm not very threatening. I told one of them when they brought me a sandwich that I needed the restroom. When I went there, I had a plan and since they untied my hands to eat. I went out the window. But Ethan—they keep drugging him every time he stirs. He's not looking good. He's gray, and his lips are turning blue."

"That sounds like oxygen depletion. Do you know what they're injecting?"

"No. It's some white liquid."

"Could be Propofol. If they're not careful, he could overdose."

"Wait—my other shoe." He reaches into the mud, fishing around.

"Where exactly were you planning to run to?"

"I don't know—a road, maybe wave down a trucker or a good Samaritan."

I sigh as he retrieves his soggy loafer. "Thomas, we're on an island. No trucks. Just water on all sides. The only way in or out is by boat or helicopter. Maybe a seaplane, but don't get your hopes up."

"So...you have a boat?"

"Yes. And it came with a SEAL."

"Oh, that's nice. You know how I love animals."

"Not that kind of seal—a Navy SEAL. You know Jac?"

"I didn't know he was a SEAL. Why wouldn't he say that?"

"He doesn't like to talk about it. I practically had to drag it out of him."

I take his arm. "We need to get back to the boat, and you have to be absolutely silent. Last I saw, Jac was near the house. We can't risk blowing our cover before Larson gets here. Stay close. Keep your hand on my shoulder. I have night vision—you don't."

"This is...exciting. Like the movies."

"Keep in mind—unlike the movies, these guys don't fire blanks, we don't fall onto inflatable mats, and getting shot is not something you just walk off."

"Okay. I'll keep my mouth shut."

"Let's—"

Thomas trips over a root and lets out a shrill yelp.

"Sorry—branch thing," he whispers, miming zipping his lips.

He's one of those people it's impossible to stay mad at.

Better to walk in silence and get back to the boat in one piece. No point grilling Thomas now when we'll have to go over it all again in front of Jac.

We'll regroup, figure out our next move, and pray the darkness holds a little longer.

Chapter 41

Got Thomas, Lost Jac

U sing the trees as cover, we creep along the water's edge. Every step threatens to slide out from under me and pitch us into the shallows. Worse than falling in is stepping on a sleeping alligator—one snap of those jaws and you'd never see another sunrise.

The ground turns too marshy to risk. We ease up the embankment, farther from the water.

Muffled voices drift from the house ahead. If we can hear them, they can listen to us. Silence isn't just smart, it's survival.

Thomas clings to my shoulder like a baby sloth. He must be terrified, but he didn't freeze back there. When he saw an opening, he took it. Braver than I'd given him credit for. I misjudged him.

My foot catches on something. I stumble and recover in the same motion, heart heaving.

"What was that?" I whisper, scanning the shadows through the green haze of my goggles. Whatever I hit isn't just debris—it slid across the dirt.

Thomas points. "There."

I crouch, adjusting for clarity. A shape lies half-hidden in the weeds. I drag it closer.

"It's Jac's ballistic vest," I breathe. "Why would he take it off?"

Panic prickles up my spine.

"Do you see him?" Thomas asks, voice shaking.

I sweep the clearing, nothing but dark shapes and the hush of the bayou.

"No. No sign of Jac." I swallow hard. "I don't like this. We're too exposed. Let's get back to the boat."

I point at the cooler. "Grab some water and something to eat if you like."

"I don't have much of an appetite. What are we going to do without Jac?"

"There's no blood. Jac didn't get shot. He left the vest on purpose. He doesn't make moves without a reason."

"You think they found him?"

I exhale slowly. "When I heard that thump at the window, tthe thugs probably came out to check. He must have let them see him so that they wouldn't come after you."

"Leave it to me to put Jac in more danger." His eyes mist over.

"You did the right thing. One less innocent in the house—and one tactical wizard in their place. I'd call that a step closer to ending this."

I take a breath. "Were there any others inside?"

"No. Just Janet, her boyfriend Joe, and those two thugs. I don't know their names—just 'bro this' and 'bro that.'"

I let out a shaky sigh. "That's a relief. I was worried the Reyes family would get caught up in this. They're a sweet couple, two kids."

"There's just the four of them. And poor Ethan."

"Shh—wait." I tilt my head. "Do you hear that? My phone—it's vibrating under the life jacket."

"I'll get it." He retrieves it gingerly, like it might bite.

"Hello?" I whisper, though I don't recognize the number.

A man's voice crackles through, tired and annoyed. "Look, I don't care what you people are doing here. I've got my own problems. I came to this place to get some peace, maybe get lucky, and not be bothered. I've been on that darn boat too long. I needed a break. So I was checking if this place was empty."

I cover the mic and whisper, "Jac must've dialed me on mute. We can hear them—they can't hear us. Don't say a word. Just listen. He's probably feeding us a clue."

Janet's voice cuts in, cool and sharp. "You didn't see the lights? Didn't think the place was occupied?"

"A lot of people leave lights on to make it look like they're home," Jac says, chuckling like he's swapping fishing stories. "Believe me, I've gotten into enough houses without getting caught."

"So you're alone?"

"Yeah, I'm alone. Check the boat if you want—nobody there."

I meet Thomas's wide eyes. "That's our cue."

I gesture to the duffel. "Take that. I'll grab the speargun."

No sooner have we scurried behind a fallen tree thick with foliage than one of the thugs approaches the boat. A light voice in my head reminds me of Jac's SEAL mantra—one second decision. I need to act deliberately, not just react. The choice is clear. We move.

The sound of Thomas unzipping the bag is enough to draw the goon's attention. It's just as well. We can't hide forever.

I stand, speargun aimed at center mass. At this range, he knows I can't miss. His weapon is across his chest—safety on. Will he risk it? Let's hope not.

"Is he here?" I ask.

"Who are you talking about?"

"The scoundrel I've been tailing—he thinks he can leave his wife and kids behind. I've been on him since he left the marina."

"So...who are you?"

Just in time to spare me further improv, he hits the dirt—Thomas's taser catches him square in the back.

"Thanks, Thomas. I wasn't in the mood to keep chatting."

I exhale. "We have to move fast. If this goon goes missing too long, we'll have company. Get the zip ties and duct tape. We've got a package to wrap." I pick up the discarded MP5 and realize it's a plastic replica machine gun. Authentic-looking, enough, but really?

I nod toward the tree line. "Let's not leave this guy too close to the water. He might not stay there long, if you know what I mean."

"Alligator bait?" Thomas grins.

Chapter 42

On Our Own

"I need to reach Larson. We have to get her ETA."

"Think you can? This place is a black hole for communications. But somehow, we could hear Jac," Thomas says, raising an eyebrow in genuine confusion.

"He has a satellite phone—best reception money can buy. I'll have to try mine. That way, when Larson chews me out for going rogue, at least I can say I tried."

I hit send, but nothing. One bar, flickering like a dying firefly. Terrific.

Alright, how do we get Jac and Ethan out before Bro Number Two comes sniffing around for Bro Number One?

A chill skitters up my spine. Something's wrong. Please let it be Jac's phone and not Jac himself.

"Thomas, do you hear anything from the house?" I whisper.

He goes still. "No. Now that you mention it, I heard some crackling—then the voices just--stopped. But my adrenaline was spiking, my ears were pounding. We were kind of busy trussing the guy up like a Thanksgiving turkey."

"There's no time to weigh options—there's only one." I strap on the oversized ballistic vest Jac left behind. "I'm going in."

"How? The front door?"

"The same way you got out. The bathroom window."

"I'll go with you."

"No. You stay here and watch the package. If he so much as twitches, zap him again. Keep the speargun ready. You do know how to use it, right?"

"Please. I'm a certified diver. I've speared more red snapper than you've had beignets. Don't worry about me—I got this."

"Thomas, you never cease to amaze me."

I'm forever thankful that when Thomas slipped out the window, he didn't bother to close it behind him. Now, all I have to do is climb in and not be tripped up by the dangling machete hanging from my belt. The window creaks open as I slide in like an anaconda stalking its prey.

The darkness inside is thick and heavy, swallowing the sliver of moonlight behind me. My hand tightens on the flare gun stuffed into my waistband. If this goes sideways—and let's be honest, it might—at least I can set the whole place on fire as a distraction.

I ease the rest of my body over the sill and lower myself to the tiles. My breath sounds too loud, too ragged. I stay crouched, listening. Nothing. No footsteps. No voices. Just the damp, musty air and the low hum of the generator out back.

I push the door open a crack. The hallway is a tunnel of darkness, broken only by the glint of something metallic on the floorboards, a spent shell casing—my pulse thuds in my ears. If Jac fired his Glock, we would have heard the shot. So it only stands to reason the bad guys fired—and they must have a suppressor on their weapon. My thumb brushes the hilt of the machete. It's not exactly a fair fight if Janet and Joe are still armed. I slide the flare gun into my palm anyway. They won't expect that.

The boards creak under my boots as I creep forward, inch by inch. Every shadow seems to twitch. Every gust of night air feels like a hand on my neck.

I pause at the threshold of the main room. Why the complete blackout? The generator is still humming; did they cut the power on purpose? If I'm lucky, they've already cut and run. If I'm unlucky—well, I'm about to find out.

I draw a slow breath, steady my grip, and step into the darkness.

I slip into the main room, stepping over an over-turned chair. The shadows seem deeper here, pooling in every corner. I'm grateful the full moon sneaks peaks through the clouds. My flashlight would give me away, but my eyes are adjusting, picking out shapes—sofa, cof-fee table, and a trail of scuff marks on the floorboards.

A muffled sound comes from the far side of the room. My heart does a little stutter-step. I freeze, straining to hear—another noise, a low rasping breath.

I follow it, moving past the cold fireplace and into the narrow hallway beyond. The door to the pantry is ajar. A soft clinking sound—metal against wood.

I nudge the door open with the machete tip.

Jac is slumped against the wall, wrists bound with nylon zip ties. His face is pale, slick with sweat, and there's a fresh gash above his temple. He blinks up at me, relief flickering across his eyes.

"You look terrible," I whisper.

He exhales a weak, humorless laugh. "You're a sight for sore eyes. They—they took Ethan."

"Where?"

Jac shakes his head. "I don't know. I tried to stop them. One of them clipped me with the butt of my own gun. I'm guessing they still have it."

I kneel beside him, cutting the ties with my handy survival knife. He winces as circulation rushes back into his hands.

"Can you stand?"

He tests his weight, nearly crumples, then braces a hand on my shoulder. "My legs are asleep. Give me a minute."

"We don't have a minute."

He looks past me toward the darkness. "Then let's make it quick. Before they come back."

Jac steadies himself against the doorframe, sucking in a ragged breath. I slip an arm around his waist, but he waves me off, determined to stand on his own.

"Where do you think they took Ethan?" I whisper.

He shakes his head, eyes scanning the darkness. "Somewhere close. They didn't have time to drag him far. But then again, I was out for a bit, hard to say for how long."

I move past him, deeper into the hallway. Every step feels like it takes a year. A part of me prays Ethan is simply unconscious—because the alternative is worse.

At the end of the hall, a slice of light spills from a half-closed door. I motion for Jac to stay behind me. He doesn't argue. I think his head injury is graver than he claims.

I nudge the door open with the barrel of the flare gun.

Ethan lies sprawled on a lumpy mattress, duct tape across his mouth. His eyes flutter open slightly. His breathing is slow—too slow—and each exhale rattles in his chest.

I hurry to his side, ripping the tape away. His head lolls against my arm.

"Ethan—can you hear me?"

A soft groan. No other response.

Jac sinks to his knees on Ethan's other side, pressing two fingers to his neck. "Pulse is weak. The drugs they've given him are taking their toll."

"We have to get him out of here," I say, voice tight.

Jac looks at me, face drawn. "If we move him too fast—"

"If we leave him, he might never wake up."

Outside, somewhere in the dark, a floorboard creaks.

I snap my head toward the sound—the night air presses against the doorway like a held breath.

"Help me," I whisper.

Jac doesn't hesitate. We brace Ethan between us, careful to support his head. My heart hammers as I listen for more footsteps. Three of them armed, three of us wounded, I think we're about even.

If Janet and Joe are still here, they'll hear every move we make. But if we wait, we may never get another chance.

We lift Ethan together and slip back into the shadows.

Chapter 43

I'd Rather Shoot Pictures

We inch back down the hallway, Ethan sagging between us. Every shuffle of his boots across the floor feels like a gunshot in the dark.

I'm halfway to the main room when a shape detaches itself from the shadows near the doorway.

"Don't move."

Janet's voice is icy calm. She steps forward, raising Jac's Glock in both hands. Her hair is plastered to her face, damp with sweat and fury. Joe emerges behind her, unarmed. That's a relief.

"Let him go," I say, my voice low but steady.

"You're not in a position to give orders," Janet snaps. Her gaze flicks to Ethan, then back to me. "He's worth a lot more alive. So here's how this is going to work—you're going to step aside."

"Not happening."

Joe's eyes were darting to the open window behind me. "Janet. We don't have time—"

"Shut up," she hisses.

Ethan lets out a weak groan. Jac's hand tightens on my arm, steadying himself.

"You don't have to do this," I say, taking a small step forward. "It's over. The FBI is already on its way."

Janet's lip curls. "Then we'll be long gone before they get here."

Her finger tightens on the trigger. I weigh my options—flare gun in my pocket, machete strapped to my side—but with Ethan half-conscious and Jac barely standing and unable to focus, there's no clean way out of this.

"Drop your weapons," she orders.

I let the machete clatter to the floor, but keep the flare gun hidden behind my leg.

Joe and the remaining thug—who must have been stationed at the dock—approach us and take hold of Ethan, who is barely able to stand.

Joe edges toward the door. "Come on. Let's move."

Janet backs away, the gun never wavering. She jerks her chin toward Ethan. "If you follow us, he dies. Understand?"

I nod slowly, though every muscle in my body is coiled tight.

They retreat step by step, inching toward the door that leads to the dock. For a second, I consider trying to shoot the flare right in her face—but with Ethan so close to them, I can't risk it.

Janet throws the door open. Cool, damp night air rushes in, carrying the distant thump of engines. The cavalry is close but not close enough.

She meets my eyes one last time. "You should've stayed out of it."

Joe and the hooded hoodlum step onto the porch. A swift swoosh cuts through the night before the hoodlum topples forward, dragging Ethan with him.

Janet fires into the darkness—two quick shots. I hope she's a lousy shot.

I run onto the porch and close the distance. I could fire from here and nail her. But I've been trained not to shoot someone who no longer poses a threat. And never shoot somebody in the back.

Janet and Joe flee toward the boat, leaving the speared ruffian behind. We still have Ethan for now.

I can only hope Thomas isn't bleeding out in the dark—and he managed to slice their fuel lines like we planned.

Because if he did, they're not going anywhere.

And that means this fight isn't over yet.

The porch boards creak under my boots no matter how lightly I tread forward, heart thudding in my throat. Beyond the dock, the boat engine sputters, then dies with a sickly cough.

Another try—nothing but a hollow grind and a sputter.

Janet's voice pierces the night, filled with rage.

"Get it started!"

"I'm trying!" Joe barks back.

I risk a glance around the corner of the porch railing. In the blue wash of moonlight, I can see them silhouetted in the boat. Janet leans over the outboard motor, cursing as she rips the cover off and fumbles with the fuel line.

I feel Jac step up beside me, one hand pressed to the gash on his head. His breathing is shallow, but he's standing.

"Thomas?" he whispers.

I scan the darkness, then spot movement near the edge of the trees. A hand lifts in a weak wave—Thomas. He's alive, flat on his belly in the mud. Relief loosens the knot in my chest for half a second.

Joe tries the ignition again. The motor gurgles like a dying frog and goes silent.

"They're stuck," Jac murmurs.

"Cornered," I correct, tightening my grip on the flare gun. "And they know it."

"They could go to the boat that was moored to the other side of the smaller dock," Jac says with a defeated look.

"I don't think so, I saw that boat untied and drifting away a while ago. Maybe Thomas? He's been a busy bee." I say, with a sense of pride.

Janet shoves Joe aside and vaults onto the dock. Her silhouette stiffens when she spots me watching. For a beat, no one moves.

Then she raises the Glock and fires.

Wood splinters explode around me. I duck, dragging Jac down behind a stack of crates as two more shots crack the air.

Ethan lets out a thin, pained groan.

"Keep her busy," Jac rasps, voice tight with pain. "I'll get Ethan under cover."

"You're in no shape to—"

"Neither are you," he snaps, the old steel in his voice sparking back to life.

I meet his eyes and nod once.

Jac crawls toward Ethan while I take in a deep breath, counting to three. On "two," I pop up and fire the flare gun.

The burning charge arcs over the dock and lands in the shallows, throwing wild orange light across the boat and Janet's stunned face.

She ducks behind a piling, cursing. Joe scrambles after her.

Somewhere in the distance, a siren wails—faint but growing.

The reinforcements are almost here.

But first, we have to survive the next five minutes. Without hesitation, I load up the next flare.

The flare's last embers gutter out, leaving darkness pressed against the windows like a held breath.

Out on the dock, Janet's voice cracks the quiet.

"It's dead!"

"I told you!" Joe yells back, panicked, lacing every word. "They cut the line—"

"Tell me something I don't know," she snarls.

I creep to the edge of the porch, keeping low. The masked thug sprawled on the planks gives a wet groan, trying to lift his head. I ignore him. My focus is locked on Janet's silhouette.

She kicks the boat's console with a hollow thud, then swings her gaze across the shoreline, searching.

"There's the other boat," she says, her voice going flat and cold. "The one that brought them here"

Joe hesitates. "Janet...we can cut our losses and live to do it again."

"—and what? Swim?" She rounds on him, shoving his shoulder. "We are not getting caught. Not after everything."

Inside, I hear Jac dragging Ethan deeper into the house. I pray he can hold out and not pass out.

Thomas's voice comes from somewhere to my left, low and hoarse. "Jess."

I flinch, then spot him crouched near the corner of the porch, one hand pressed to his ribs.

"You all right?" I whisper.

"Clipped. Not deep." He jerks his chin toward the dock. "They'll search the shoreline. Your boat's next."

"My thoughts exactly."

Out by the water, Janet steps off the deck and starts stalking down the narrow spit of sand that curves behind the house. She sweeps the muzzle of the Glock across the shadows, hunting.

Joe hangs back, glancing at the porch—at me. For a heartbeat, I can feel his eyes like lasers trained on mine. Sometimes, when there is so much hate, you may not see it, but you can feel it.

"She's going to get us killed," he mutters, almost too soft to hear, but the water is such a wonderful conductor.

He looks like a man defeated and ready to bolt.

I ease the flare gun up, just enough that he can see it if he's thinking of trying the porch stairs.

His gaze flicks to the weapon. He doesn't challenge me.

Thomas shifts closer, keeping low. "We need to move. If she finds that boat—"

"—We're done," I finish.

I nod to the masked thug writing on the boards. "Can you cover me?"

Thomas flexes his injured arm and grimaces. "I can try."

"Good enough."

I slip back through the doorway, heart hammering. Jac is propped against the wall near the pantry, Ethan sprawled at his side. Jac's face is pale in the dim light.

"Didn't they have another gun? One with a suppressor, there was a spent shell." I ask, wondering why Janet has taken over Jac's Glock.

"Oh, that. Joe had it, he dropped it, safety off, it fired and jammed all in one motion. It was almost comical. Amateurs." He says with a crooked smile.

"She's searching for the boat," I say quietly. "It won't take her long."

"We could let them take it, if they can. Help is on its way. They won't get far."

"Oh no, I won't let that happen. It's a matter of principle." I say.

Jac swallows. "Then you'd better get there first."

I bend beside Ethan, pressing two fingers to his throat. His pulse is thready but steady.

"You hold here," I tell Jac. "If she doubles back, you barricade the door."

He nods once, jaw tight.

I slip out the side door, hugging the wall as I circle the house. The night is alive with insect chatter and the distant thrum of engines still too far away to save us.

Ahead, Janet's silhouette moves along the sand, her flashlight beam slicing the dark. She's maybe fifty yards from where Jac's skiff is hidden under the natural tree canopy.

Close. Too close.

Chapter 44

Flaring Up

I draw a deep breath, steady my grip on the flare gun, and start creeping after her, one careful step at a time.

I move in a crouch, each step sinking into the damp sand. Ahead, Janet's flashlight beam flicks across driftwood and scrub, searching for the outline of the skiff. She's muttering to herself, voice ragged.

"Where are you...where the heck..."

I can hear Joe behind her, lumbering along the beach. He's had enough—of this, of her, of everything.

When Janet reaches the curve in the shoreline, she stops short. Even in the darkness, I see the moment she spots the tree overhang over the boat.

"There," she breathes.

She picks up her pace, boots crunching over the twigs and dead branches.

I break cover, circling wide, staying low behind a tangle of palmetto and brush. My heart is hammering so loud I'm sure they'll hear it.

Joe catches up to her, glancing over his shoulder. "Janet—let's just—"

"Stop, already," she snaps. "Help me get it free from this mess."

Joe hesitates, then crouches to tug at the branches.

I slip closer, close enough to hear the wet rasp of their breathing. The sirens are louder now, winding up the labyrinth of waterways—still a few minutes away.

Janet rips branch after branch and tosses them aside. The moonlight glints on the aluminum hull of Jac's boat.

"Keys," Joe pants. "Do you even have—"

Janet whirls on him, eyes wild. "Do you think I didn't plan for this?"

She fishes in her pocket, yanks out a small bundle of keys.

I can't wait any longer.

I step out of the shadows, flare gun leveled. "Don't move."

Janet goes rigid. Joe looks at me like he's been handed a reprieve from the devil herself.

"Put it down," I say, voice calm, cold. "It's over."

Janet's gaze flicks from me to the boat, to Joe—and back again. Her hand tightens on the Glock.

"Jessica." Her tone is almost gentle. "You don't want to do this."

"You're right. I'd rather be anywhere else. But here we are."

The sirens wail closer, echoing off the water.

Joe swallows hard. "Janet...she's right. We're done. Let it go."

Janet's jaw tightens. For a heartbeat, I see the calculation in her eyes—the math of desperation.

Then her lip curls.

"No."

She raises the Glock.

I fire.

The flare roars out of the barrel, a comet of blazing red. It hits her square in the chest, erupts in a bloom of fire and sparks.

Janet screams—a high, ragged wail—and drops the gun as she flails at the flames. Joe stumbles back, hands raised.

I rush forward, grabbing the Glock, tucking the flare gun back in my belt, and yanking the flare torch free of her jacket before it ignites her completely. She collapses to her knees, gasping.

Joe drops to the ground, palms out. "I'm done. I swear—I'm done."

Behind me, headlights break through the trees. Boat engines rumble, closer now, and the thumping blades of a helicopter churn the air overhead.

I keep the Glock trained on them until blue lights strobe across the beach.

It's finally over for now.

Chapter 45

Sunrise On The Bayou

Blue strobes pulse across the beach, washing over Janet as she hunches on her knees, arms wrapped around herself. Joe stays flat in the sand, breathing in ragged gulps.

Agents swarm in from the tree line, weapons raised. One of them barks orders I can't quite process over the blood rushing in my ears.

A hand closes over my shoulder—Thomas, limping but upright. His face is pale, streaked with sweat and grime.

"You good?" he rasps.

I nod, though I'm not sure that's true. My arms feel like lead. My heart is still galloping.

Two agents pull Janet to her feet and snap cuffs around her wrists. She doesn't fight them. Just stands there, staring past the waves, as if she finally understands it's over.

Another pair dragged Joe up. He doesn't resist, eyes vacant.

Off to my right, EMTs converge on the masked thug writhing in the sand, the spear still embedded in his thigh.

"We'll need an evac for this one," one shouts over the wind. "Possible femoral involvement."

They start working quickly, cutting away fabric and prepping a stretcher.

Footsteps crunch behind me. I turn as Jac emerges from the brush, a couple of agents supporting Ethan on his unsteady legs. Ethan's face is slack and gray, but when I step closer, his eyes flutter open.

"You...made it," he whispers.

"Yeah," I murmur, voice thick. "We all did."

The wind picks up as the first helicopter descends—red cross on the side, rotors kicking up grit and shredded leaves. EMTs hustle to load Ethan onto a stretcher.

A second helicopter circles in behind it, the Night Sun sweeping the clearing. The door slides open, and a familiar voice crackles over the loudspeaker.

"Well, Jessica, are you ready for those beers? " Slick drawls.

"More than ready." Despite everything, a short laugh breaks out of my throat.

The medic chopper lifts first, Ethan safely aboard, followed by the speared thug strapped down and sedated. The engines roar, shaking the trees.

"Wait!" I yell. "Thomas is going with you. He caught a bullet."

"I'm okay. I can go back on the boat with Jac," he says, stiffening his shoulders.

"I know you're my hero, and you saved the day more than once. However, you need to let them treat you. You let these medics do their best, and I'll see you soon."

Thomas exhales, sagging a little as the EMTs guide him toward the chopper.

As Bayou Six-one copter settles into place, a tall silhouette steps down—Special Agent Larson, headset in place, eyes scanning the scene. She meets my gaze and gives a slight nod that says we've got this now.

I feel the last knot in my chest loosen.

Larson strides over, boots a bit unsteady in the sand. "Jessica, you're coming with us. I want your statement, and I'm pretty sure you want to get home as soon as possible and catch about twelve hours of sleep."

"Don't suppose there's coffee on board?"

Slick leans out of the cockpit, grinning. "We'll see what we can scrounge up. But first—let's get you out of here."

"Larson, we found another one." An agent calls out.

"Another what?" Larson answers utterly confused.

"Another perp hogtied in the bushes."

"Oh yes, I almost forgot about him. Thanks, agent, for pointing him out." I wave at the agent gratefully. And turn to address Lora, "He's one of the infamous four. Glad the agent found him. I can assure you my intention was not to leave him behind to feed the gators."

"Are you sure?" Lora asks with a smirk.

"By the way, do yourselves a favor, have him ride on one of the boats going back, downwind, he got tased," I yell at the agent who found him and is in the process of cuffing him.

"Thanks, I see the problem." He waves back and moves him towards one of the boats.

"Jac, come along. I'm sure they can get the boat back to your place."

He takes one last look back, shaking his head, then walks toward the chopper.

I look one last time at the dark water, the flickering lights, the evidence markers appearing scattered through-out as the silhouettes of the forensic team take form and the first rays of light rise above the horizon.

Climbing into the chopper, my spirits lift, grateful to witness another sunrise on the Bayou.

Main Characters in Bad Blood in the Bayou 'Wide-Angle'

Jessica Martin

Renee Dolton

Ethan Fontaine

Jane Douth

Janet Jones

Special Agent
Larson

Jac

Thomas Dupris

Elias Collins
Slick

T.K

T.C.

Also by this Author

WRITE NOW! It's Never Too Late
The Path to Personal Success and Freedom
Creativity Business Plan for Artists and Artists as Heart
Live the Life You Love; Seizing Your Success
Chloe's Journey (Illustrated Children's Book)
Bad Blood in the Bayou 'FRAMED'
An LA to LA Cozy Mystery Book 1
Coming Soon!
Bad Blood in the Bayou 'FREEZE-FRAME'
An LA to LA Cozy Mystery Book 3
Read Chapter One of FREZZE-FRAME
let me know your thoughts.

Acknowledgements

Books don't write themselves, and authors don't grow without the support of many. Huge thanks to my author friend Sharmyn McGraw for keeping the gremlins at bay. To my friends and family for cheering me on and laughing at my wild ideas. You're the wide-angle lens that makes the picture complete.

Bad Blood in the Bayou 'Freeze-Frame'

An LA to LA Cozy Mystery Book 3

Chapter 1

Snow in the Bayou?

I never thought, in my wildest dreams, I'd see my beloved Crescent City covered in snow. The French Quarter looks like a Thomas Kinkade painting—gas lanterns flickering behind frozen panes, rooftops cloaked in white.

Going to photograph Evette Larue's mansion might be an impossible challenge for some under these conditions. However, with my trusty Jeep Trailhawk, I should be able to traverse the roads and do some interior shots. The dreamlike light drifting through the tall windows is too perfect to pass up.

It's been two days since the blizzard brought up to ten inches of snow. Now the roads are clearing, the snow slowly retreating under the sun—and the locals' irrepressible warmth.

I'm not sure how TK and TC feel about their sweaters, but since they're curled up together, I'm going to call it a win.

Speaking of warmth, Evette's call this morning to make sure I'd be safe on the road, was so sweet. She's such a dear. I assured her I'd be fine—and reminded her she'd braved the trip herself from the Quarter to the mansion. She, of course, matter-of-factly informed me she had to be there. As she wanted to check for any damage from the snowstorm. Words, she said, she never thought she utter, living in Louisiana.

I have my equipment, my boots, and I have to laugh as I pull on my hooded quilted red jacket—like some jolly elf about to go sled-riding. So glad this snow will be short-lived. While it's here, one must rejoice and take advantage of its beauty. I'm determined to get some photos of the Bayou before it melts away. But for now, let's get to the supposed haunted mansion.

"Bonjour, Mon Cher," Evette says, arms open wide, her air kisses warm despite the cold.

I linger in the foyer, removing my boots before I go any further. To my surprise, she's ready for me with a pair of fluffy slippers. She insists I wear them, apparently, the floors are chillier than usual.

"I swear," she says, shaking her head, "this place is chilly even in July. Air-conditioning or not, it never warms up.

"Before you start, you must have some hot tea. I won't take no for an answer."

Who am I to argue? And knowing Evette, she wouldn't let me lift a camera until I'd had tea and her special French pastries.

After the welcome and the tea, finally, it's time to work. I take stock of the place, the atmosphere, letting my creative mind envision the shots before I ever touch the shutter. Sometimes I see a setting as moving pictures. Other times, a freeze frame in time.

I'm eager to discover what this assignment will uncover.

Like my mom always said whenever she cleaned the house—start at the top and work your way down. So, let's start in the attic.

I may not have to photograph the area, but you never know what treasures might work their way in the shot.

Attics are fabulous troves of discarded and once-cherished items—priceless to someone, sometime in the past. And sometimes still relevant, whether we realize it or not.

The dormer window casts a soft, diffused light across the floor. The room seems larger than it should be. Naturally, there's a rocking chair in one corner.

My heart gives a stupid little jump. If that thing starts rocking on its own, I'm flying down the stairs, fluffy slippers and all.

All right. Let's find a light switch before I spook myself further.

I grope for a string and, as I tug it, stub my toe on a box. Not much protection in these frivolous slippers.

Light spills across the room, and the shadows shift and settle. My eyes catch on something scrawled in bold black letters across the lid of a filing box:

COLD CASES

I don't believe in coincidences. Or maybe I do, more than I'd like to admit. Because those words drew me in like a magnet.

Who left this behind? Whose cases are these? Whose lives are still frozen in time, because no one ever found closure?

Gosh, I sound like an owl. Maybe I'll have the wisdom of an owl to find justice. Perhaps, not for everyone—but if I can help just one, it'll be worth it.

My heart hammers as I slide the dusty and musty lid off.

On top of the files lies a framed picture of a young girl in a white winter coat, surrounded by snow. A faded yellow sticky note clings to the glass.

April 12, 1997—D.T.

I can't leave this here. If I do, it won't just haunt this attic it'll haunt me.

The End...for now

Check back at www.JulieBelmont.com
for updates, publishing date for this book in the Series of Bad Blood in the Bayou 'FREEZE-FRAME'
An LA to LA Cozy Mystery Series Book 3, and other happenings that you want to follow.

About the author

Julie is an eclectic creative with a flair for weaving intrigue into both words and art. As a storyteller, she delights in crafting cozy mysteries filled with charm, suspense, and just enough mischief to keep readers turning the page. A seasoned writer and visual artist, Julie balances her time between pen and brush, capturing characters and scenes with the same keen eye she brings to her mysteries.

When she's not unraveling fictional puzzles, Julie shares her life with rescue pets and does her part to care for the world they all call home—tidying beaches, tending trails, and respecting Mother Earth in quiet, meaningful ways.

Her life, much like her stories, blends creativity, compassion, and a touch of the unexpected.

In Closing

Thank you for reading the second book in the
LA to LA Cozy Mystery Series.
I hope you found it enjoyable and entertaining.
To keep updates on my work, please visit my website
www.JulieBelmont.com
Please write a review, even a short one, where you
bought your copy.
You're the key to this book's success!
Gratefully,

Julie